A Wonderful Adventure

Part four

The Battle for Earth

Prometheus

Published by
Chipmunkapublishing
United Kingdom

http://www.chipmunkapublishing.com

ISBN   978-1-78382-7374

I dedicate this latest adventure with Jonny Plumb to you, the person reading this book.

Prometheus

Jonny Plumb's jaw-dropping adventures continue in rip-roaring fashion with his latest book, Jonny Plumb and the Battle for Earth. Jonny and all his friends set out to save the Earth from the evil clutches of the devil's only daughter, Deadsheda, and her henchwoman, the even uglier and more revolting Dances with Death, who has a strange aversion to custard. I wonder why? Read as the Outriders from Hell try to break the force field created by the Shard of Pure Light to destroy Jonny, his family, and friends and steal the Golden Globe. Watch Nanny Noo take on Deadsheda in unarmed combat. Yes, one ageing nanny fighting the most evil, hideously ugly, cackling devil child. Will she win? Will Nanny Noo be the hero? Will all Jonny's friends and family join together as one with Blueshadow and the Water Horses from Jala, the planet of pure water, Firestorm and Starshell, along with Dentro Reclu and the beings of Pure Light, to help Nanny Noo, Jonny, Legion, and Legend save the Earth?
Read in nail-biting horror as the Gnud Repeek threatens to return to destroy Jonny and allow the devil to reign supreme over all humanity. Please sit back and

enjoy the ride of a lifetime with Jonny Plumb and all his friends.

CHAPTER ONE:
DANCES WITH DEATH

'Jonny, Jonny, wake up and let me in,' Isobel whispered.

Jonny slowly opened his tired, sleep-filled eyes and looked around his bedroom, wondering if he had heard Isobel's voice or if he was still dreaming. Suddenly, it dawned on him that he wasn't lying in his bed but floating a few inches above it.

Jonny then began to float slowly higher and higher, and the more he struggled to get back to the safety of his bed, the higher he climbed. Suddenly, out of the corner of his eye, he saw a dark metal grill in the ceiling and wondered how long it had been there, as he had no memory of ever seeing it before.

Jonny struggled to turn his head and look down. After some great exertions, he saw Legion and Legend still fast asleep next to his bed, totally oblivious to what was happening to him.

'Jonny, help me,' Isobel whispered again, her voice calm and, as always, beautiful.

Jonny wrestled with all his strength against the seemingly invincible invisible power that was gently and ever so slowly lifting him closer and closer to the eerie, dark metal grill in the ceiling.

'Jonny Plumb, you must save me,' Isobel said quietly, but her voice seemed slightly more strained this time. Then, Jonny realised that Isobel's voice was coming from behind the grill, not from where he assumed it was coming from, behind the bedroom door. Jonny's heartbeat

7

quickened as he struggled harder and harder to free himself from this invisible force, which gently but now quite forcefully pushed him higher and higher and closer and closer to the dark metal grill. Jonny tried to shout 'HELP' to the sleeping Legion and Legend, but there was only silence as Jonny's voice was lost. As Jonny got closer and closer to the dark metal grill in the ceiling, he felt a cold chill all over his body and a smell so evil that he almost choked.

'Jonny, please, Jonny, please,' Isobel begged. Isobel's innocent voice suddenly turned into that of a cackling and evil entity that screamed,
'Keep away!'

Jonny's face was now directly under the dark metal grill, and the stench was so overpowering Jonny thought he would pass out. He struggled to push himself away from the ceiling, but his body seemed rigid with paralysis, unable to move anything but his head. Jonny's body rose a few inches until his nose touched the ice-cold, dark, insipidly gloomy grill.

Jonny began to shake uncontrollably with absolute fear and terror as beads of sweat trickled down his face, making a quiet 'thump, thump, thump' as they hit the softness of Jonny's bed. Legend and Legion slept on, unaware of Jonny's torment in his wide-awake nightmare.

'I love you, Jonny Plumb,' Isobel whispered. Then, suddenly and without warning, Isobel's face appeared behind the dark metal grill, making Jonny jump out of his skin. The beads of ice-cold sweat drip effortlessly onto Jonny's bed's softness, 'thump, thump, thump,' as they hit the pristine white sheet.

Isobel's usually beautiful, fair, and delicate skin suddenly darkened; cracks appeared around her soft mouth and beautiful eyes. Isobel's nose began to bleed as green and purple pus oozed out of her mouth and slowly dripped onto Jonny's face.

Jonny retched repeatedly, his body caught in spasms of absolute fear. He watched as the girl of his dreams slowly transformed from the most beautiful girl in his world into the most hideous, vile creature he had ever seen. Isobel's hair had now turned from a shiny chestnut brown into a dying grey.

Crawling amongst it, bloated maggots emerged from her skull, chewing and munching at the living flesh.

Jonny tried to scream with every ounce of strength, but his voice stayed silent. He desperately tried again and again to free himself from the all-powerful force that held his body against the ceiling.

Isobel's once beautiful face was now unrecognisable. Her face, now green and purple, had enormous pus-filled slashes that suddenly opened down her once pristine cheeks. Isobel began to smile; her teeth morphed into razor blades, and her once pink tongue flicked in and out of her pus-filled mouth, swollen with sores like a snake tasting the air of its next victim.

Suddenly, she screamed at the top of her voice like a raging banshee.

'Jonny Plumb, you are mine forever, mine, until the end of time.'

Isobel then clamped her rotting, razor-blade teeth onto the metal bars as her rotten breath of death enveloped Jonny's face. The bloated maggots dropped from her evil, foul, stinking mouth into Jonny's. Slowly, ever so, she began to rip the bars apart. Bit by bit, the ear-screeching terror got closer and closer until her crooked, bent, pus-filled nose touched Jonny's.

'OH MY GOD, HELP ME,' Jonny screamed as he finally found his voice.

Jonny turned his face from side to side, desperately trying to move away from the death breath and hideous vision before him. The invisible, powerful force just pushed it back, but this time, even closer to the hideous hag's pus-filled and achingly ugly face in front of him as it cackled.

A gnarled hand suddenly reached out of the darkness and grabbed Jonny's head. Silently and with unstoppable force, it dragged Jonny into the attic's cold darkness.

'OH MY GOD, PLEASE GOD, PLEASE SAVE ME,' Jonny screamed out in terror as he felt his head being dragged into the dark coldness of the attic while the once beautiful Isobel screamed repeatedly.

'Today, you are going to die; you are going to die, today, in hell.'

Jonny, still sweating and shaking with fear, suddenly realised that his body was beginning to fall. Slowly, his head emerged from the darkness of the attic, further and further away from the foul stench of death and the hideous face grinning inanely at him. Blood, pus, and maggots continued to fall towards him.

Jonny kept falling in slow motion, sweat pouring from his entire body. Silently, Jonny landed on his bed with a thump.

'Jonny, wake up, Jonny, you must wake up,' a soft voice whispered. Jonny tried to open his eyes, but something was covering them. He reached up tentatively and felt Pod's warm, silky fur. Then, he felt the soft breaths of Legion and Legend nuzzling up to him.

'It's ok now, Jonny, it's all over,' the reassuring, chocolate-melting voice of Nanny Carole whispered, her beautiful scent filling Jonny's nostrils.

Jonny opened his eyes and looked directly towards the ceiling. Then, he nervously and silently scanned the entire bedroom ceiling, looking for the dark metal grill.

'What on earth were you dreaming about, Jonny? You woke the entire house up,' Legion asked.

'It was horrible, just horrible,' Jonny stuttered.

'What was?' Carole gently asked as she stroked Jonny's face.

'The face, the face behind the grill in the ceiling,' Jonny replied in near hysteria.

Legend, Legion, and Nanny Carole looked up towards the ceiling where Jonny was pointing.

'There, it was there, believe me, I saw it, and Isobel was trapped behind the grill and had changed into a hideous witch,' Jonny stuttered.

'But there's nothing there, Jonny,' all three repeated together.

'Guess you have just had a horrible nightmare,' Nanny Carole said gently.

'Yes, I guess so,' Jonny replied, still looking shaken, 'I guess so.'

'Someone at the front door, Jonny, asking for you,' Nanny Carole said while tidying Jonny's room and straightening the bedclothes.

'Who's at the front door?' Jonny asked, still uncertain about the nightmare he had just woken up from.

'Are you ok, Jonny?' Legion asked sympathetically.

'Well, to be honest, no, I am not,' Jonny replied while cuddling up to Pod.

'I thought you would have grown out of needing Pod,' Nanny Carole whispered.

'Pod is my emotional strength; Legion and Legend are my physical strength. Without these three, I am nothing.'

'So, who is at the front door?' Jonny added as he unsteadily stood up and slipped into his slippers.

'Oh yes, almost forgot, it's Big Chief Runny Stool,' Nanny Carole replied.

'Big Chief, what?' Jonny asked, giggling.

'No, not Big Chief what, but Big Chief Runny Stool and his daughter, Laughs at Parps.'

'You have got to be joking,' Jonny replied, still giggling, repeating, 'Laughs at Parps.'

'No, I'm deadly serious. If you don't believe me, then go and see,' Nanny Carole said as she continued to make Jonny's bed.

* * * * * * *

Legend, Legion, and Jonny ran down the three flights of stairs to find a very old-looking Native American and his stunningly beautiful daughter sitting cross-legged in the hall. A bemused Nanny

Noo observed from behind the safety of the kitchen door.

'He, he, hello,' Jonny stuttered as he walked over to the two seated Native Americans.

There was silence, no reply, no sound, no movement, not even a flicker of life.

Jonny looked to where Nanny Noo was hiding and raised his hands, gesturing to say, 'What is this, then?' Nanny Noo shrugged and continued peeping from behind the kitchen door, safe.

Legion sniffed the Chief and then sniffed the Chief's beautiful daughter, Laughs at Parps.

'Well?' Jonny asked.

'Yes, thank you,' Legend replied.

'No, not you, him?' Jonny said, pointing at the cross-legged, ancient-looking man in the hall.

'I think they are both fast asleep,' Legend added.

'Or dead,' Legend said, laughing.

'Well, best wake them up then,' Jonny said, prodding the Chief.

'Hold on, how did they get in?' Nanny Carole asked as she descended the stairs carrying the week's washing.

'Well, didn't you let them in?' Jonny asked.

'No, I thought you did.'

'How could I have let them in? Remember you told me about them when I was in my bedroom with you? And how do you know their names?' Jonny asked.

Suddenly, Big Chief Running Stool and his daughter, Laughs at Parps, began to float approximately one foot into the air. They then floated through the large oak doors and into the empty lounge, back into the hall, and then into the kitchen, pushing the door and Nanny Noo gently out of the way. Then they both floated up the stairs, followed closely by a very curious Jonny, Legend, and Legion.

'What's making them move?' Nanny Noo whispered while still hiding behind the safety of the kitchen door.

'Oh, I think I know,' Legend replied, pretending to hold his nose and pulling a toilet chain.

'Oh, no wonder she is called Laughs at Parps,' Jonny said, giggling as an almost silent phutt, phutt, phutt came from Big Chief Running Stool and Laughs at Parps' bottoms. Suddenly, all hell broke loose as Big Chief Running Stool and Laughs at Parps let rip a silent but lethally deadly parp and suddenly moved at the speed of light.

'Oh, I wish I could do that,' Legion said.

'You do, and you do often. The only difference is you don't float,' Legend replied, laughing.

* * * * * * *

Jonny, Legend, and Legion ran up the three flights of stairs in hot pursuit of the floating, parping Native Americans and stood in the doorway of Jonny's bedroom. Suddenly, the tray of one hundred phials floated effortlessly from under Jonny's bed.

Without warning, a hundred phials lit up in a fantastic light show, and then Big Chief Running Stool, his daughter, Laughed at Parps, and a hundred phials all began to sing. Suddenly, a crack of lightning was so loud it made Legion and Legend howl in pain, which was immediately followed by an incredible thunderclap, making the entire house shake.

'They're here,' Laughs Parps said quietly as the tray containing the one hundred phials slowly and effortlessly floated back under Jonny's bed.

'Who's here?' Jonny asked while calming Legend and Legion. Suddenly, two more massive cracks of lightning smashed into the invisible force field, and once again, it was followed by an even louder thunderclap, which shook the foundations of Jonny's home.

Jonny leapt up and peered out of his bedroom window. He was astonished by what he saw as more massive lightning bolts slammed into the force field surrounding Jonny's home and garden.

* * * * * * *

 'Has anybody seen Isobel?' Jonny asked nonchalantly as he walked into the kitchen, ignoring the ear-piercing lightning cracks and deafening thunderclaps.

'Quick, everybody, to the caves,' Sir Ranulf shouted.

'Not until I find Isobel,' Jonny shouted, trying to be heard above the tremendous noise of thunder and lightning strikes and the rain that now fell in torrents.

'Charlie, go to the caves and see if Isobel is there, will you, old boy?' Sir Ranulf shouted at the top of his voice.

'And take Legend and Legion,' but Sir Ranulf's voice was lost in the incredible noise of the worst storm.

Legend and Legion lay down, shaking, while trying to cover their tender ears from the painful, piercing lightning strikes as they repeatedly hit the force field that protected all from within.

'Where do we keep the cotton wool?' Jonny shouted.

His words were lost as the noise of the world's worst storm got louder and louder and more ferocious.

'Will the force field hold?' Professor Ziad shouted.

'I think it best if you all went into the caves,' Jonny shouted back. 'Half past eight,' the Professor replied.

'No, I said go to the caves,' Jonny repeated while pointing towards the door in the kitchen.

'Yes, it is,' Professor Ziad replied while taking the shaking hands of Philomena and Nanny Noo, soon followed by Lady Kathleen, Charlie, Nanny Carole, Sir Harry, his wife Bunty, a floating cross-legged Big Chief Running Stool, and finally Rabbcat.

'Just me and you then,' Sir Ranulf shouted.

'No, Dad, you must go as well,' Jonny implored, pushing this six-foot-six-inch giant of a man towards the cellar door.

'Not leaving you alone, son,' Sir Ranulf bellowed.

'Oh, yes, you are,' with one rapid manoeuvre, he pushed Sir Ranulf through the cellar door and slammed it shut.

The storm's noise suddenly increased as Jonny tried to find something to help Legion and Legend cope with the ear-piercing, screaming lightning strikes.

'Bingo,' Jonny shouted as he found the old first aid box. He carefully pulled out the cotton wool and a couple of the old crepe bandages and quickly placed bundles into Legion and Legend's bleeding ears. Jonny knew they were both stone deaf, so that conversation wouldn't be easy. Jonny gave Legend and Legion the thumbs up and mouthed, 'Is that alright?'

'YES, IT'S PERFECT,' they both shouted back so loudly it almost knocked Jonny clean off his feet.

'We have to find Isobel,' Jonny shouted and realised the boys couldn't hear a word as they had cotton wool stuffed into their ears.

Laughs at Parps grabbed Jonny's hand as he ran, and she floated into the vast back garden, which was almost pitch black, dark as a raven's wings at midnight, and deathly silent. The thunderstorms and lightning flashes momentarily ceased, and eerie silence was around the darkness.

'Jonny, are you ready?' Spirit asked.

'No, not really, father,' Jonny replied.

'To overcome the bad, we must join as one,' Spirit added.

'Who must join as one?' Jonny asked wistfully.

'You, your mother, and I,' Spirit said gently.

'But if we become one and are beaten, then it is the end,' Jonny replied.

'Yes,' was Spirit's solitary reply.

'Well, what about the rest? Firestorm, Starshell, Dentro Reclu, the Beings of Pure Light, and Cosmos, not forgetting the parping power of Flatulent Philomena,' Jonny added, but sadly, his sense of humour was lost.

'Jonny, we are the only ones who can save them, this world, and all the worlds in the multiverse. Do you not understand, Jonny? This is the final battle, my son. We were chosen, chosen because we have lived so many lifetimes. You alone spent one hundred years learning from the nine Planets of

Wisdom. You have forgotten more than most know. Your wisdom and strength are unparalleled.'

'What about?' Jonny stammered while looking at the ground and then at Legion and Legend. 'What about Legend and Legion? I can't leave them. I was promised that they would be with me forever. You can't tell me they will not be with me; you can't do that to me.'

Jonny began to weep uncontrollably and repeated. 'No, you cannot take away my best, most loyal friends. I will not allow anyone to take away Legend and Legion. No one, and I mean no one, not even you, Father, not even you.'

'What did he say?' Legion shouted at Legend. Legend shrugged his shoulders, unable to hear a word.

Legion gently undid the crepe bandage wrapped around Legend's head, and then, in turn, Legend gently returned the favour.

'Now, Jonny, what were you saying?' Legend and Legion asked in unison.

'I have to leave you,' Jonny said while wiping the steady stream of tears from his face.

'Never, we will never leave you; we vowed to you that we wouldn't ever leave you,' Legend and Legion replied in unison and then added.

'There are three of us: Legend, Legion, and Nerrac. There are three Gods in Pashoo: Spirit, Cheroo, and Jayzu. There are three stars in Orion: Mintaka, Alnilam, and Alnitak. The universe has three Gods: the Father, the Son, and the Holy Ghost. We are one, we are the same, and we are life. We are one, I am you, and you are me.'

'So be it,' Spirit replied, 'so be it.'

* * * * * * *

Once again, there were three loud bangs, accompanied by shouts from Sir Ranulf.

'Jonny, open this bally door,' Sir Ranulf screamed. Jonny ran back inside, straight into the kitchen, and stood beside the cellar door.

'Father, I cannot let you out,' Jonny said quietly.

'Stand back, laddie,' Sergeant Rockhard's familiar gravel voice boomed. Within seconds, the cellar door swung open, and after a few seconds more, the dust clouds had disappeared. Sir Ranulf, Harry, Charlie, Professor Ziad, Mac, and a few soldiers from Eddie's regiment stood there.

'If you think you are going into battle alone, laddie, well, you had better start thinking again,' Eddie quietly said while sitting at the kitchen table. A steady stream of heavily armed soldiers ambled in, sitting, standing, brewing tea. Soon, Nanny Noo, Nanny Carole, Lady Kathleen, and Philomena walked in, followed by many men, women, and children.

'We're not leaving, Jonny,' they all said in one voice.

Jonny wasn't sure whether to laugh or cry. Laugh from sheer joy of seeing his loved ones again, or cry through fear of losing the family he so loved.

'Chinese parliament,' Eddie said calmly.

'We need a very clever plan, Jonny,' Sir Ranulf said, smiling, 'a very, very clever plan.'

'Does the radio work?' a voice echoed from a distance.

Jonny picked up his radio and turned the dial, but nothing was static. He quickly turned the tuning dial; still nothing, just static.

'Try another wavelength, Jonny,' Sir Ranulf urged. The radio fell silent.

'What's happened to everyone?' Nanny Noo said, with real fear in her voice.

Suddenly, a bang on the front door made everyone jump with fright.

'Who on earth could that be?' Lady Kathleen asked as Sir Ranulf, accompanied by Sir Harry, went to the front door. Standing in a black cloak that looked like it was made from the universe, there was a tall, shadowy figure of a man.

'I need to speak to Jonny,' the mystery man said in perfect English, his eyes ablaze with love and understanding.

Sir Ranulf and Harry stood motionless, open-mouthed, just gaping at the tall, dark, incredibly handsome man standing in the doorway.

'Jonny, is that you, Jonny?' Sir Ranulf stuttered.

There was silence for a few fleeting seconds as Sir Ranulf and Sir Harry exchanged silent but knowing glances.

'But that's impossible,' Sir Ranulf blurted out, his knees weakened by the pure shock of what he was looking at.

The man walked in—well, actually, he didn't exactly walk in; he floated in. Standing open-mouthed and silent in the hallway were Lady Kathleen, Nanny Noo, Nanny Carole, Charlie, Professor Ziad, Philomena Fudge Bucket, Legend, Legion, Eddie, and not forgetting Jonny.

There was silence. You could have heard a parp on Mars; it was so quiet.

Lady Kathleen started to weep openly as she recognised the tall, dark, handsome man in his floor-length cloak, who had the universe in his hands.

'Son?' she asked while grabbing the arm of Charlie to stop her from fainting. 'No, this is impossible; this just cannot be.' And slowly, as if in slow motion, she passed out right next to Nanny Noo, who had passed out unnoticed some minutes earlier.

Jonny stood open-mouthed as the man stood and stared back. 'Hello Jonny, do you know who I am?'

Still stunned and unable to utter a sound, Jonny shook his head.

'I am you.'

There was a thud, then another, and then another. 'Will you lot stop fainting,' Sir Ranulf barked out.

'My husband,' a quiet voice came from the back of the crowd.

'My wife,' the man replied, and out of the crowded kitchen floated Laughs with Parps, with tears streaming down her face and her body trembling. She ran towards the man with the universe in his cloak, and they embraced.

'What on earth is happening?' Jonny whispered to Legend.

'Well, to be honest, Jonny, I am a bit lost for words, but if that's you in the future, that can only mean one thing: you must have won the greatest battle of all time, and if Laughs with Parps is your wife in the future, then what happened to Isobel?'

'Eddie, can you sort out the crowds of people? My house has become a commune, and I need my home and family back to some normality,' Sir

Ranulf said gently, adding, 'We cannot allow the women and children to join in the forthcoming battles.'

'Why not? We can fight as hard as the men,' a voice shouted.

'Correct, but we need you to care for the children, the food, and the animals. Have you ever seen a man cook?' Sir Ranulf said, laughing.

'Yes, good point,' the voice replied.

Soon, the kitchen had emptied and returned to a semblance of what it once looked like.

'OK, anyone for tea?' Nanny Carole asked while helping Nanny Noo and Lady Kathleen to stand up.

'I must talk to you all as I cannot stay,' the mysterious man said, sitting down. His cloak, filled with the universe, glittered and turned everything it touched to a soft glowing light.

Everyone sat down and listened intently to his words.

'Yes, Jonny, I am you. I am Jonny from the future, and I have returned to tell you how to destroy the evil that has already caused worldwide death and destruction. Jonny is the only one who can do this, and it is, without a doubt, the most dangerous mission you will ever undertake, and it is one that Jonny must do alone.

First, we must save Isobel, and then Jonny must somehow get to Amaranta. He must get there on a specific date, at a particular time, when all the planets are in alignment. This must be done at the precise time without knowing what the time is. Failure to complete this hazardous mission will mean the end of all life, and I mean all life on Earth, on Pashoo, and in the known multiverse.'

'No pressure then, Jonny,' Charlie chuckled.

'But you being here, doesn't that mean we conquered all evil?' Lady Kathleen asked.

'No, it just means that I am here right now, and I will soon be gone,' Future Jonny said in a matter-of-fact tone.

'Oh well, that's about as clear as mud,' Sir Ranulf said, scratching his head.

'Ok, so why can't I get to Amaranta?' Jonny asked.

'Well, do you have the Shard of Pure Light, or did you hand that over to Blueshadow? And what about the Golden Globe? Do you have the Golden Globe?' Future Jonny asked Jonny.

'Well, erm, no,' Jonny replied.

'Then how do you intend to get into Amaranta? If I remember correctly, young me, you cannot even get out of the safety of your garden, let alone fly in the Silver Flying Arrow.'

Legend nudged Jonny and whispered, 'Tell yourself about, you know, the flying and being invisible.'

'But if he is me, he will know that won't he?' Jonny whispered back.

'Good point, good point. Ok then, how did he get here? Because if he can get in here, he must be able to get out, so perhaps ask him,' Legend replied.

'You want me to ask myself?' Jonny paused and added, 'Hold on a second, what if I... no, that won't work either because I can't leave here, can I?'

'Oh, you can leave here, but you won't be able to get back. Well, not until the force field made from the Silver Shard of Pure Light is removed, and you can only remove that from the inside,' Future Jonny replied.

'So, let me get this right. I have to leave here, but I can't because of the force field made from the Silver Shard that Blueshadow now has. Then I have to get to Amaranta and do something I don't know about yet, in total darkness, at a certain time when all the planets and stars of the universe are in alignment on the right day, the right hour, right minute, and to the precise second, without knowing the time or date, also, on my own, without Legion and Legend, and all without being seen or caught by Deadsheda or the Gnud Repeek. Then I must return and get back into the safety of my home, which I can't leave or, for that matter, get back into because of the force field. So basically, I cannot do anything. Did I miss something? Perhaps I have to go naked with a giant octopus on my head as well.'

'Yes, apart from the giant octopus and the naked bit,' Future Jonny said, smiling, and then added, 'Remember what you have already learnt and probably forgotten on Bodha, the planet of knowledge about light.'

Jonny thought for a minute while wracking his brains. He raced through one hundred years of gained knowledge and came up with just one idea. 'I need a bath,' he exclaimed. Then, he disappeared up the stairs to run a bath and think about how he would make the impossible possible. But before he could go, Future Jonny held Jonny's hand and whispered something into his ear. Future Jonny then handed over the Cloak made from the Universe and, with a massive smile, turned to all the assembled and said, 'I must now return,' and without uttering another sound, vanished into thin air.

'What did he whisper, Jonny?' Legend asked.

'A number and a secret,' Jonny replied, disappearing up the stairs, quickly followed by Legion and Legend.

* * * * * * *

Soon, the bath was full, but the water was ice cold as there was no longer any gas supply. Jonny gently touched the ice-cold water, and instantly, it became a rainbow of colours and became beautifully hot.

'Oh crikey, I forgot all about Isobel!' Jonny shouted out. 'Come on, Legend, come on, Legion, we have to find Isobel.'

* * * * * * *

Jonny ran into the kitchen to organise a search party but then realised that if Isobel had been taken before the force field was put in place, then he would not be able to get her, not until he somehow found a way to penetrate it, which he had no idea how to do.

'Eddie, take a few of your men and scour the caves,' Sir Ranulf asked calmly.

'Do you have a picture?' Eddie asked.

'Strange time to ask for a photo of me,' Jonny replied, smirking.

'Aye, very funny, laddie, but if you could be serious for one minute, do you have a photo of Isobel?'

'No, but I can describe her. Shoulder-length brown hair, brown eyes, with a few freckles on her face just below her eyes,' Jonny replied.

'What about her clothes? What was she wearing the last time you saw her?' Eddie shouted back from just inside the cave entrance.

'A flowery dress and—' but before Jonny could finish his sentence, Eddie and his men were gone.

'Last night you had a nightmare,' Nanny Carole said in her melted chocolate voice.

'THE ATTIC!' Jonny shouted and whispered, 'Oh, the attic,' as he remembered last night's horrid nightmare. 'Oh no, not the attic,' he repeated.

* * * * * * *

Legend and Legion nuzzled up to Jonny to reassure him that he wasn't alone as they all looked up at the attic door. Jonny picked up the six-foot metal rod with a T-shaped hook on the end, carefully slotted it into the T-shaped slot, and gently pulled. Nothing happened; it would not budge. Jonny tugged a little harder until he pulled with all his might. Still, the hatch wouldn't budge. Then Jonny tried again and pulled so hard the metal T-shaped hook snapped clean off, propelling Jonny across the landing floor. Suddenly, the loft door slowly began to open, creaking as it did, and the old, battered wooden staircase began to descend independently. Legend and Legion lifted their noses into the air and began to sniff, their hackles jutting up from their backs like spears. The old, battered stairs continued to fall as if in slow motion, and then they gently hit the landing rug. Then, a cold wind blew out of the attic, making the goose pimples stand up on Jonny's arms and skinny little legs, but this cold wind had an evil stench. Legend and Legion stood stone still, staring into the dark void of the attic, both growling a growl so low it made the walls and floor vibrate.

'Help me, Jonny, help me,' whispered Isobel, and Jonny froze in fear as Legend and Legion edged towards the bottom of the rickety old stairs.

'Help me, Jonny, help me. There is something up here with me, Jonny,' Isobel's faint and feeble voice repeated.

'I don't like this,' Legion whispered as he turned to face an ashen-faced Jonny.

'No, nor do I,' added Legend.

'No, no, nor me,' Jonny stuttered, his little skinny knees knocking together in fear.

'Yeah, what is that awful smell?' Legend asked, lifting his massive head and sniffing at the putrid smell from the attic.

'Jonny, please help me, help me. Oh, Jonny, please help me; I am so alone and scared. Help me, Jonny.' Isobel's voice sounded tired and weak.

'I have to go,' Jonny said bravely, but before he could put his scruffy plimsolls onto the first step, Legion and Legend ran past him at full pelt, growling ferociously as they managed the thirteen steps in three bounds and into the dark void of the attic. Jonny ran up the steps and stood motionless, staring into the darkness.

'About time you turned up, Jonny Plumb, as you are just in time to DIE,' screeched this vile voice from the depths of the freezing attic.

'Where's Isobel?' Jonny demanded, trying to ignore the foul stench and the hideous creature slowly floating out of the green mist towards him. Jonny instantly recognised the hideous, green-faced, bloated, gut-wrenching, pus-filled boils, hook-nosed and deranged, staring-eyed hag, which floated effortlessly towards him as Dances with Death.

'Where's Isobel? Tell me, or my dogs will eat you,' Jonny shouted.

Legend looked at Legion, and Legion looked back at Legend, and both silently mouthed, 'Eat her! I would rather suck on a nappy.'

'Your silly dogs cannot harm me, Jonny Plumb, because I am already dead, and even you, Jonny Plumb, cannot kill the dead. But you can make me stronger by eating your soul,' Dances with Death cackled as green pus splashed everywhere.

Legend and Legion started to growl, louder and louder, as Dances with Death floated backwards and forwards as if she were attached to a swing while dancing the danse macabre.

Suddenly and very slowly, she began to turn her head as her neck bones clicked, click, click, and there, hidden under her grey cobweb hair, was another hideous face. She slowly turned her head again to reveal another repulsive face, even uglier than before. Jonny stood open-mouthed as Dances with Death turned her neck full circle. The gut-wrenching noise of her neck breaking almost made Jonny faint.

'That's the most revolting sight I have ever seen,' Legend said, feeling like he was about to be sick.

'Looks like she put her make-up on with a brick,' Legion added.

'Machete, more like,' Jonny quipped, trembling, and then added, 'So you are three and not one? One plug-ugly, stinking, rotten, diseased corpse.'
'Yes, we are. We are the dead, and we will devour your very soul,' Dances with Death replied, her voice changing to encompass her two achingly revolting twins of evil.
'WHERE IS ISOBEL?' Jonny shouted.
'IN HERE,' Dances with Death replied while rubbing her bloated stomach, 'IN HERE.'
'I have to end this, and I have to end this now,' Jonny whispered to Legion and Legend, standing a few inches away from the still swaying, cackling, revolting Dances with Death.
'I agree, but how? We cannot kill her as she is already way past dead,' Legend replied.
Jonny thought momentarily, trying to remember all the tricks he learnt while he was on Bodha, the planet of learning, and then said, 'Bingo, gut buckets,' and whispered into Legend and Legion's ears.
'Run downstairs and ask Nanny Noo if she has these five ingredients: eggs, cornflour, milk, vanilla, and caster sugar.'
'Have you lost your marbles?' Legend and Legion replied in unison, then started to laugh.
'What are those two poodles laughing at, and why would you want eggs, cornflour, milk, vanilla, and sugar?' Dances with Death shouted back, spitting green vomit from her revolting mouth.
'CUSTARD,' Jonny, Legend, and Legion all replied.
'C-Cu-Cus-Custard, did you just say that word, CUSTARD?' Dances with Death stammered.

'Oh yes, we certainly did say, CUSTARD, because you like custard, don't you, you evil, parping, grotty-granny?' Jonny replied, smirking. In an instant, Legend and Legion ran downstairs to the kitchen.

'I hope the odious devil-child Deadsheda is more intelligent than you three sad acts because,' Jonny said, paused momentarily to give the second part of his sly and cunning plan time to work.

'Because what?' the impatient, visibly annoyed, and frightened Dances with Death replied.

'You don't like it when people ignore you, do you? Or when they are not frightened of your hideous face. I also know that you do not like the word C.U.S.T.A.R.D. You are also trapped, but you were so busy being revolting and hurting Isobel that you forgot one tiny thing. Well, apart from the fact that I know you hate custard.'

'We can leave whenever we want,' Dances with Death cackled.

'Oh, ok then, off you go then,' Jonny said calmly while looking at his fingernails. Dances with Death scanned the dark attic, looking for a way to fly out.

'You still here?' Jonny said, smiling.

Dances with Death suddenly realised the reason she couldn't leave. She was so intent on trying to scare Jonny and, worse still, stupid enough to fly into Jonny's attic to hide that she didn't reckon on the immense power of the Silver Shard of Pure Light. She was trapped because no one could leave, especially the cackling, vomit-faced evil called Dances with Death.

Dances with Death tried to move. She screamed out all her evil rage and ordered her broom to obey. It didn't.

'Listen, you vile, ugly, cabbage-smelling, spotty, parping bint, you are trapped as the Silver Shard of Pure Light is far more powerful than you could ever imagine,' Jonny said, grinning.

Suddenly and silently, a steady stream of hot custard arrived, quickly carried up the four flights of stairs by a constant stream of happy volunteers.

'Custard, custard, let's kill the evil witch with custard. Custard, custard, let's kill the evil witch with custard,' they all chanted. 'Custard, custard, let's kill the evil witch with custard.'

The large bowls of piping hot custard were carefully placed around the warty, gnarled, stinky feet of Dances with Death.

'C, C, CU, CUS, CUST, CUSTARD,' Dances with Death stammered.

'Yes, c, c, cu, cus, cust, custard, you anvil-headed monkey butt,' Jonny replied.

Jonny picked up two bowls of freshly made piping hot custard and aimed them straight for Dances with Death's hideous faces. Then he picked up two more, and soon, everyone was throwing piping hot bowls of yellow custard.

'Good shot,' Sir Ranulf said as Lady Kathleen hit Dances with Death in the face with a bowl of hot custard.

'Oh, this is such fun,' Philomena Parpy Fudge-Bucket said, throwing bowl after bowl at lightning speed.

'Didn't you have sprouts for dinner last night, my little puff adder?' Professor Ziad asked his diminutive wife, who was so busy enjoying herself she could hardly reply for giggling.

'Yes, I ate about a week's worth,' she replied, still giggling and chucking bowl after bowl at the now custard-soaked Dances with Death.

'Well then, my little sugar dumpling, parp for England,' Professor Ziad said, quickly putting a tea towel around his face.

'Just brewing up a real humdinger of a stinker,' Philomena added.

'NO, NOT THE CUSTARD, NO, NO, NOT THE CUSTARD PARPS,' Dances with Death screamed as Jonny and everyone else continued to throw bowl after bowl of hot custard into Dances with Death's grot-ridden, pus-filled, scabby, old faces. Then, right on cue, Philomena lived up to her name and let rip.

'PAAAARRRRRRRRRRRRRPPPPPPFRAPPPAR PFRAPPPPPPPPARPOO.'

'Oh my God, that has to be the vilest, smelliest, tongue-curling, headshaking, knee-knocking, vomit-inducing, belly-aching, head-spinning toilet burp I have ever had the misfortune to hear and smell,' Jonny said, rolling around the floor in absolute hysterics.

Suddenly, as the custard parp took effect, she began to change. Her grey hair started to fall out in huge clumps, and her vile skin started to sag.

'My hair, my teeth, my eyes, I'm not beautiful anymore,' she whined, as bit by bit, lump by lump, eyeball by eyeball, her revolting face began to fall onto the dusty attic floor, making a hissing noise as it dropped.

'Help me, Dead Sheda,' were Dances with Death's last words before the only thing remaining of Dances with Death was her broom and a ring made from bone. Sadly, there was no sign of Isobel, and Jonny's heart sank.

'Quickly, open the skylight and get rid of this awful smell before I pass out,' Jonny shouted.

Legend and Legion checked every corner of the attic, looking for signs of Isobel, while Jonny looked at the odd ring made from bone. It had an inscription, but Jonny couldn't figure out what it was due to the poor light. Instead, it looked like an initial.

'What do we do with that?' Legend asked, pointing at the heap of old custard-drenched clothes that was once Dances with Death. Before Jonny could reply, it simply vanished into thin air, cleansed by the power of the Silver Shard of Pure Light.

Pleased with their handiwork, everyone meandered back to the kitchen to work on plan B, seeking and destroying DEADSHEDA.

Jonny silently closed the attic door and breathed his first breath of fresh air.

* * * * * * *

'Anyone seen Laughs with Parps?' Jonny asked.

'Come to mention it, I haven't seen her or Chief Runny Gruel, er Chief Gummy Botty, er, Bunny Rissole,' Sir Ranulf replied while looking under the kitchen table.

'No, they both disappeared when future Jonny turned up,' Nanny Noo said while washing the last saucepan.

'Why does everyone keep disappearing?' Jonny asked, then added quietly, 'Which reminds me, where is Isobel?'

'Well, she's not in the caves,' Eddie said as he and a few armed men walked purposefully back into the kitchen.

'Can you get any signal from your walkie-talkie?' Sir Ranulf asked Eddie as he finished a very ripe and delicious peach.

'The batteries are all but flat, so we need some power,' Eddie replied, stuffing another peach into his face.

'Try Genevieve,' Jonny shouted.

'Yes, of course, why didn't I think of that,' Sir Ranulf and Eddie replied in unison.

* * * * * * *

Sir Ranulf opened the front door and was taken aback by the serenity. Everything was still and calm, the sky a stunning blue, and there was silence, not a single noise.

'Eerie,' Eddie said, then muttered, 'the quiet before the storm.'

'Sorry, what was that you said, old boy?' Sir Ranulf asked.

'Och, it's nothing, but there is something in the air; can you not feel it?' Eddie replied in his deep Glaswegian accent.

'Yes, come to think of it, it is quite creepy, but I was trying to keep a stiff upper lip and not let it get to me.'

Sir Ranulf opened the garage doors, put the key into the ignition, and instantly, Genevieve purred into action. Eddie quickly wired up his two-way walkie-talkie and almost passed out with shock when he heard a young woman's soft, gentle voice.

'Help me, help me,' the voice echoed weakly.

'There is a girl's voice,' Eddie whispered to Sir Ranulf and Jonny while holding his gnarled hands over the receiver.

'Ask her name,' Jonny replied.

'This is Sunray Alpha; please repeat your name over,' Eddie gently asked.

'Isobel.'

'Sunray Alpha to Isobel, please repeat, over.'

'Isobel.'

Jonny grabbed the walkie-talkie and shouted down the receiver.

'Isobel, can you hear me?' Jonny waited and waited and then asked again.

'Isobel, can you hear me?'

'Yes, but only just,' Isobel whispered.

'Where are you, Isobel?'

'I don't know, but I feel safe, warm, and floating, Jonny.'

'Floating? What, in the air like Mary Poppins or...'

'No. Floating in a beautiful multi-coloured sea,' Isobel butted in.

'JALA,' Jonny shouted, jumping up and down.

'Isobel's at Jala.'

'Where the bally hell is Jala, old boy? Is it near here?' Sir Ranulf asked calmly.

'No, No. It's near Pashoo, which means,' Jonny suddenly went quiet and whispered, 'Which means the evil didn't destroy my star parents' home planet or its inhabitants.'

'Isobel, Isobel, how did you get there, and are you alone?' Jonny said, hardly able to contain his excitement.

'NO, SHE IS NOT ALONE,' an evil voice screamed and suddenly, the line went dead.

'No, No, Isobel, Isobel, come back, Isobel,' Jonny shouted, but there was no response, just crackling static.

* * * * * * *

'Legend, where's Firestorm, Starshell and my star parents?' Jonny asked as he sat down in the kitchen.

'Here,' came the reply.

Suddenly, out of thin air, Jonny's star parents, Cosmos, Starshell and Firestorm, appeared.

'I have some good and some bad news. Isobel says she is safe and is swimming in the seas of Jala, but it appears that' Jonny paused for a second before stuttering, 'She is not alone.'

Starshell looked at Firestorm, and then Firestorm looked at Cosmos, who then looked at Spirit, then at Cheroo, and then back at Jonny. Suddenly, Eddie's walkie-talkie came to life, making everyone jump and Philomena parp very loudly.

'Jonny, Jonny, come and save me,' the gentle, sweet voice of Isobel wafted from the walkie-talkie.

'See, I told you, she is there,' Jonny said forcefully, trying to make a point.

Jonny waited for reactions from those gathered around the kitchen table, a smile, or anything else. There was nothing.

'What's the matter? I thought you would be happy,' Jonny said mournfully.

'Jonny, that wasn't Isobel,' Firestorm said gently and then paused momentarily, concerned about what he would say next.

'Jonny, that wasn't Isobel; that was the infinite evil called Dead Sheda.'

Suddenly, the entire house began to shake; plates fell from the Welsh dresser; cups and food-covered plates fell off the large kitchen table, crashing noisily to the floor. Soon, the shaking stopped apart from Philomena Flatulent Fudge—Bucket, who trembled like a leaf, parping incessantly. Then, the loudest clap of thunder ever started smashing all the windows in the house as a thousand shards of razor-sharp glass flew across the room.

'Everybody down,' Eddie shouted, but his voice was lost in the tremendous noise, and then Legend and Legion's worst fears returned. Lightning after lightning strike smashed mercilessly into the protective shield surrounding Jonny's home and garden. Jonny picked up the old cotton bandages and, without thinking or looking, swiftly wrapped them around Philomena's face, leaving her gasping for air.

'Psst, Jonny over here,' Legend said while trying to stop wetting himself while laughing at the state of Philomena.

'Oops, sorry,' Jonny replied quickly, removing the bandages from Philomena's shocked, blue face.

'I thought she looked better with them on,' Professor Ziad said in a loud voice, trying to be heard above the noise of the thunder, but much to his embarrassment, the thunderstorm fell silent as he spoke. 'De De Deadsheda?' Jonny mumbled.

'Yes, Jonny, she is closer than we think. We must prepare ourselves,' Firestorm said quietly.

'How?' everybody replied as one.

'Well, first, we must destroy her, like Jonny destroyed Dances with Death.'

'What, with custard?' Jonny asked.

Suddenly, the walkie-talkie returned to life with Deadsheda screaming in her evil demonic voice.

'Death by custard, death by custard.'

'Chinese parliament,' Eddie and Sir Ranulf said in unison.

Everybody sat down and began to talk about the next plan of action as the thunderstorm raged louder and more violently, and lightning cracks smashed into the protective shield.

'That shield, it will hold. Won't it?' a very worried, knee-knocking Nanny Noo asked.

'Yes, old girl,' Sir Ranulf said reassuringly.

'And if it doesn't?' Philomena asked, still trembling.

'Don't worry, it will,' Jonny replied.

'Where are the candles? We will need some light in here, plus some heat in the lounge,' Lady Kathleen asked, wrapping her cardigan tightly around her.

'Found them, oh well, actually only found two,' Nanny Noo replied.

'I know how to produce light, and I think it's the only way I can get out of the protective dome and fly to Amaranta,' Jonny whispered.

'What did you say, Jonny, you know how to create light?' a startled Eddie asked.

'Yeah, it's easy; what you do is you collapse an air bubble underwater with a sound wave, and that produces light,' Jonny replied, beaming, then added, 'I learnt that on Bodha, the Planet of Knowledge.'

'Wibble wobble wabble,' Professor Ziad said, slapping himself around the face. He added, 'You can make light, but that's impossible.'

'Ok, want to bet?' Jonny replied.

'YES,' everyone replied; even the people in the chalk mines shouted 'yes' as one.

'Right then, what do we have to make bubbles?' Jonny asked.

'Blowing through a tube,' Nanny Noo suggested.

'Philomena,' Professor Ziad said out loud.

'Yes,' Philomena replied, thinking he was about to ask her a question.

'No, old cabbage, I wasn't going to ask you a question, just making a suggestion,' Professor Ziad said, smiling.

'What! Do you want me to stick my bottom into a water bath and make bubbles? Philomena growled.

'Only after you have eaten the odd few tons of sprouts,' Lady Kathleen said, laughing.

'No, I won't. I refuse,' Philomena replied, turning bright red and stomping her size four shoes angrily on the ground.

'Come on, old girl, you know how much you enjoy sprouts, and you can parp for England,' Professor Ziad said, nudging his still, bright as a beetroot wife in the ribs.

'Found some,' Charlie shouted.

'Found some what? Sprouts,' Lady Kathleen said, still giggling at the idea of Philomena parping into a bath.

'No, some candles,' Charlie replied.

'Oh, thank God for that. I thought you were seriously there for a minute and expected me to break wind in the bath.'

'WE WERE,' everybody replied, laughing.

'Well, before it gets dark, I'm going to have a bath and test out my theory,' Jonny said and disappeared upstairs, followed closely by the ever-present Legend and Legion.

'Ok, let's get a roaring fire going and settle down for the night and sort out what we are going to do next,' Sir Ranulf said as he ushered everyone into the lounge.

* * * * * * *

Jonny walked into the bathroom, and with a touch of his index finger, the multi-coloured water immediately warmed up to a beautiful, soothing temperature. The light was fading fast, so he knew he didn't have long to see if his untested plan would work.

Suddenly, all the sea life appeared, jumping and leaping, diving and flying in and out of the water.

'Sloppy Botty, I need you to parp, and I need you to parp a lot,' Jonny said, smiling.

'Oh no,' all the sea-life replied, 'not more parping.'

'But you are always telling me off, and now you want me to parp to order,' Sloppy Botty replied, wondering why he was being asked.

'Don't think, parp,' Jonny said, urging some movement in Sloppy Botty's bottom.

Sloppy Botty started to grimace as he brewed up a real humdinger.

'No, Sloppy, I want bubbles, not stink rot bottom burps,' Jonny said, giggling.

'Oh, for God's sake, how can I separate stink from bubble on earth?' Sloppy Botty asked.

'Quickly,' everybody replied.

'So, what is all this about?' Wall Eyed Wally asked.

'I'm going to make light,' Jonny replied.

'No, you're going to stink out our home,' the sea-life replied in unison.

'Ready,' Sloppy Botty shouted.

'Hold on a minute. You haven't explained how Sloppy Botty's bottom burps will produce light. It stinks, yes, but is it light?' Wall Eyed Wally asked.

'I will sing, I will sing at the bubbles,' Jonny replied innocently.

'Have you cracked?' Legend butted in, trying to stifle his laugh.

'Listen, if I can produce enough light to light up the house, then I can produce enough light and use the energy to escape to Amaranta, silly.'

'Oh yes, of course, silly, silly stupid, dumb, thicko silly me, imagine not knowing that,' Legend replied, slapping himself around his head with his giant paw.

'Yes, as I have mentioned before, Legend, you do the scary tough stuff, and I will do the brainy stuff. Rescue and save the world and universe,' Jonny replied.

'Excuse me, but if you don't mind, I am about to explode,' Sloppy Botty shouted.

'Oooooooops, sorry, Sloppy,' Jonny replied.

'So, Jonny, you are going to stick your silly head into the water and sing to Sloppy Botty's parping bottom, are you?' Legion asked.

'Yep, that's the idea,' Jonny replied.

'Wow, you are brave,' Squelch said, climbing out of the bath, soon followed by Wall Eyed Wally, Stench, Carcass, Harpoon, and Legs as the rest of the sea life disappeared from view and the oncoming stink.

Sloppy Botty was ready to explode when all hell let rip as he dropped the loudest, vilest, stinkiest, smelliest, toe-curling, teeth chattering, eyebrow-raising, nose dripping, knee shaking, all singing and dancing parp ever known.

Jonny held his nose, put his head under the bath water, and shouted at the top of his voice. As his voice hit a billion bubbles emerging at some speed from Sloppy Botty's parping bottom, in a millisecond, there was a massive flash of incredible brilliant white light so powerful it threw Jonny clean out of the bath. It hurtled Sloppy Botty deep into the multi-coloured waters. The light shone magnificently for what seemed like ages and then slowly dimmed.

'Do it again, do it again,' Legend and Legion said in near hysterics of pant-wetting excitement.

'Sloppy, are you ready?' Jonny asked, standing up from the other side of the bathroom and picking up Wall-Eyed Wally, Squelch, Harpoon, Stench, and Carcass, who were all hanging off the bathroom light.

'Where's Legs?'

'Over here,' Legs replied as he climbed out of the toilet. 'Oh yes, that was brilliant.'

'No, it wasn't,' Legs replied, 'it was smelly.'

'Ok, after three,' Jonny said to Sloppy Botty.

Again and again, Sloppy Botty parped as if his entire life depended on it, and again and again, Jonny shouted at the billion bubbles, and again and again, brilliant light filled the bathroom.

'Whoooohooooooo, this is fun,' the entire sea life proclaimed, except for Legs because every time

Jonny shouted at the bubbles, Legs landed perfectly inside the toilet bowl with a splash. Jonny picked himself up again and climbed back into the bath. 'Want some more?' Sloppy Botty asked.

'NO, NO, NO,' everyone replied.

Jonny quickly washed himself, jumped out of the bath, changed, and ran downstairs to tell everyone the incredible news: light from parps. Who would ever believe that?

* * * * * * *

Jonny walked into the lounge, where a beautiful fire was burning. Four candles lit the room, making shadows dance on the walls. Jonny started to laugh to himself.

'Care to share the joke?' Sir Ranulf asked.

'Oh, it's nothing, just four candles,' Jonny replied, still grinning from ear to ear.

'Four candles? What's so funny about four candles, Jonny?' Lady Kathleen replied.

Nobody understood the joke, so Jonny sat beside the roaring fire, still smiling to himself.

'Oh yes, very funny. Can I have fork handles on my birthday cake?' Nanny Noo said, giggling.

'She crouches between the radishes and peas,' Professor Ziad laughed.

Soon, everyone cottoned on to the silly jokes, except for Philomena.

'Sprout darling?' Professor Ziad asked, trying to stifle his laughter.

'I don't think me having the galloping runs is very funny and certainly not appropriate,' Philomena replied, still angry at being asked to drop a parp in a bath.

'Did your plan work, Jonny?' Sir Ranulf asked, still laughing.

'Oh yes, but we will have to do something about the smell,' Jonny replied, holding his nose and pretending to flush an imaginary toilet chain.

'Well, we could always leave Philomena in the garage if she begins to smell too much,' Professor Ziad replied, nudging the still-seething Philomena.

'Oh, come on, darling, lighten up. It's the world's end in a few days, and you're still angry about a little parping.'

'We could give you a hose next time,' Lady Kathleen smirked.

'You're not going to stick a hose in my bottom, and I don't care if it's the end of the world or not; I am refusing point blank.'

'It's okay, you silly old worrywart, darling. We are only playing with you. Of course, we wouldn't do that,' Professor Ziad replied, wiping the tears of laughter from his face.

'Oh, thank God for that because I thought I would have to eat sprouts until I was fit to burst so that you could all have a jolly good laugh at my expense. I mean, what did you expect me to do, spend the entire night with my bare bottom in a bath parping for Britain while Jonny sings, "There she blows"?'

'One thing did cross my mind, Jonny. Why are you creating energy to get to Amaranta when you have eleven spaceships in the shape of Nemesis just waiting outside?' Professor Ziad asked.

'Well, I can and will use Nemesis, but when I get to Amaranta, I need to get inside the great pyramid to set off the pulse detonator. But I can't set off the pulse detonator without finding it, and I can't find it without being inside the great pyramid. I don't have the key to the great pyramid because the key is the Silver Shard of Pure Light, and as you are all aware, it's what's now protecting us. So, the idea is that I must travel to Amaranta at the right time of day and the right second when all the planets are in alignment to set off the pulse detonator. Then, I must get back here before I leave, as the pulse detonator will level just about every man-built structure on Earth. So, to recap, I need to make the energy required from inside Nemesis and push me invisibly through fifty feet of solid stone. I hope I land in the right place at the right time and have enough light to see what I'm doing. And to be honest, the chances, however, are twofold: slim and none.'

'How long have we got until Deadsheda arrives?' Lady Kathleen asked.

'Unsure, but I must get to Amaranta and back before she gets here, as she is one powerful child and plugs ugly. One look into her mouth can kill,' Jonny replied.

'What's in her mouth that can kill?' a shaken Nanny Noo asked.

'Well, you're not going to like this, but she has a beast inside her mouth that ate her tongue and sits inside. When she opens her mouth, this hideous creature has eyes that can burn through steel, a poison so powerful that just one tiny minuscule drop can kill an entire population, and just for good measure, it's hideously revolting. It's called the Cymothoa Exigua. So, if you meet her, ensure you don't kiss, look at, snog, or talk to her. Keep well away,' Jonny replied.

'I wonder where she is now?' Nanny Noo asked, trembling with fear.

'I'M HERE,' the cackling, evil, demented voice of Deadsheda rang out from nowhere, making everybody jump.

'It didn't come from here,' Eddie said while checking his walkie-talkie.

'Well, where did it come from?' Nanny Noo said, almost passing out with fear.

'Jonny, we are safe here, aren't we? I mean, inside the Shard of Pure Light's energy?' Sir Ranulf asked, getting quite agitated.

'Nothing evil can pass through the energy field, and I mean nothing,' Jonny replied, trying to reassure a quite frightened group of people.

'But what if it was inside Isobel? Wouldn't that allow it in? I mean, she's disappeared, and this evil, well, I can feel it in my bones. I wouldn't say I like it. I don't like it at all,' Nanny Noo said, trembling.

'Nanny, if this evil, runny-nosed big job was inside Isobel, then she wouldn't get through the energy field, would she?' Jonny replied.

'Death by custard, death by custard, Isobel loves custard,' Deadsheda repeated, her evil voice laced with hate.

'We're not frightened of you,' Nanny Noo shouted, raising her gnarled fists.

'Not yet, Slim, not yet', Deadsheda replied, and then she giggled and giggled.

Suddenly, all the candles went out, and the fire died.

'Quickly, put some more logs on the fire and relight the candles,' Lady Kathleen said, her voice raised with tension and fear. Charlie tried to light the candles, but they wouldn't light. He then loaded log after log onto the dying fire.

'Listen, everyone, don't let this evil upset or scare you. She can't do anything from where she is, but I would prefer it if Firestorm, Starshell, and Cosmos went into the chalk mines, as I think it would be safer. Come to think of it, I think you should all go,' Jonny said in a matter-of-fact tone.

'Yes, I agree,' Nanny Noo replied, taking Nanny Carol's hand and quickly disappearing through the door to the caves, soon followed by Firestorm, Starshell, Cosmos, Lady Kathleen, and Philomena.

'If you need light, I'm happy to parp; I mean, help,' Philomena said as she walked through the door to the caves.

'That's my girl,' Professor Ziad said, kissing his wife.

'Okay, now there is only us left. We need to make a plan, and I need to fly to Amaranta. I need to go soon,' Jonny said.

'How much time do we have?' Eddie asked, tapping his watch, which seemed to have stopped. He tapped it again and then showed it to Sir Ranulf.

'Good grief,' Sir Ranulf replied as he checked his watch, then Charlie's and Sir Harry's. They had all stopped at precisely the same time: six seconds and six minutes past six.

Sir Ranulf picked up his torch and checked the grandfather clock in the hall, the kitchen clock, and then his bedroom clock. He checked every clock in the house, and all had eerily stopped at precisely the same time—six seconds, six minutes past six.

A chill wind made him shiver as he stood alone in his bedroom. He hurriedly closed the window and went to draw the curtains. He looked out the window at the stillness of his beautiful back garden and then checked the skies to see a formation of clouds resembling a gigantic child's face; it was the evil face of Deadsheda.

Sir Ranulf quickly closed the curtains and made his way downstairs, but his torch suddenly died, leaving Sir Ranulf in complete darkness. It was so dark that he couldn't see his hands in front of his face or the stairs in front of him. He began to feel faint and unsteady on his feet.

Suddenly, out of the darkness, he felt the powerful presence of Legend and Legion on each side of him. He grabbed their collars and was gently and reassuringly guided back to the lounge.

'You OK, old boy? It looks like you've seen a ghost,' Sir Harry asked, poking the fire, which suddenly sprung into life, and the four candles suddenly lit by themselves.

'She, she's here,' Sir Ranulf stuttered.

'Who's here, old boy?' Sir Harry and Professor Ziad said in unison.

'That thing, Deadsheda,' Sir Ranulf replied quietly and added, 'Jonny, what time do you have to be at Amaranta, and how are you going to achieve this impossible task?'

'I don't know, I don't know the correct time or, come to think of it, how many hours I have left.'

Eddie jumped up and ran outside just as the sun was setting. He placed his large, outstretched hand in front of his face and measured how far the sun was from the horizon; it was one full hand's width. He ran inside and asked the date, which everyone knew because it was June 6th.

'OK, well, the sun sets at 21.13 hours, so now it must be 20.13 hours,' Eddie replied.

'Well, I have to get to Amaranta today, but I still have no idea what time,' Jonny said.

'Did you not say it was when all the planets were in alignment?' Professor Ziad asked.

'Yes, but not only our nine planets but those of the Sombrero Galaxy as well, and the only person who knows that is Spirit.'

Suddenly, two balls of light appeared, lighting up the dim lounge, and Spirit's voice boomed out.

'My son, you must be at Amaranta at midnight tonight. It would be best if you went alone, but it has been agreed that you can take Legion and Legend. Be safe, my son, be safe.'

'Well, that's a relief, eh boys,' Jonny said while playing, fighting with Legion and Legend, who both whispered, 'We would have gone with you anyway.'

'So, I need to get Nemesis up and running. I also need a large tank of water and a hosepipe, and I must remember the codes to set off the pulse detonator, which I don't know,' Jonny said excitedly.

'Jonny, the code is the prayer,' Spirit said.

'Yes, yes, yes, I knew it, I just knew it,' Jonny said, jumping up and down.

Charlie came in with ten feet of garden hose and an old tin bath. 'Bucket,' Sir Harry shouted.

'I beg your pardon,' Sir Ranulf replied, laughing.

'Bucket, we need buckets, buckets of water as I doubt if the Nemesis carries any, and there won't be much in the desert, will there?' Sir Harry replied.

Charlie reappeared with ten buckets; luckily, these ten buckets all had lids.

'OK, so we have a hosepipe, ten water buckets and a large egg timer,' Eddie said, 'now what else?'

'Egg timer? Jonny won't have time to boil an egg, Eddie,' Sir Ranulf said, laughing.

'Yes, what's with the egg timer?' Sir Harry asked.

'To tell the time, silly,' Jonny, Sir Ranulf, Eddie and Professor Ziad replied in unison.

'Oh yeah, silly me,' Sir Harry replied sheepishly.

Eddie ran outside to the garden just in time to see the sunset; as soon as the sun disappeared, Eddie turned the egg timer to allow the sand to start to fall.

'OK, Jonny, this egg timer takes thirty minutes to empty. It is now 21.13, so how many times have you turned it?'

'Oh, that's easy, five times,' Jonny replied.

'Yes, laddy, but what about the spare seventeen minutes?'

'I will count it down.'

'Well, good luck with that old boy as you will be rather busy producing light, finding the pulse detonator, then reciting the Lord's Prayer while counting down to the exact second, not forgetting that you have to be back before you leave,' Professor Ziad said while smiling.

'My boy can and will do that,' Sir Ranulf said, reassuring a quite nervous Jonny.

'Yes, yes, of course I can.' Jonny replied. 'Of course I can.'

* * * * * * *

Jonny, Eddie, Charlie, Sir Harry, and Sir Pinner stood beside the Nemesis and giggled at this amazing machine's ridiculous size and immense power. They then looked skywards to see the evil cloud formation and quickly averted their gaze. Silently, a small doorway opened, and Jonny quickly placed the old tin bath, the ten buckets full to the top with water, the hosepipe, and the egg timer inside and slowly waited until the last grains of sand had fallen. Jonny then turned the egg timer upside down again, knowing he had just thirty minutes before he could leave. Jonny worked out in his head how all this was going to work, how he had to fill the bath, create the bubbles by blowing very hard and then shout at the top of his voice to generate enough light to power him through forty feet of solid stone to the precise place, to recite the prayer and get out again and home by midnight—some task. Suddenly and without warning, all hell broke loose as lightning strike after lightning strike smashed into the protective light shield. Enormous storm clouds filled the night sky, and the Outriders from Hell came out of the dark.

Four-winged, black-as-midnight horses pulled chariots of fire across the night sky, and Death rode on the chariots. Thousands upon thousands of the dead rose from their graves to fight the last battle on Earth. They screamed, and they screamed a terror song so powerful that the entire shard of pure light protecting the house shook as the chalk caves began to crack. Jonny stood transfixed by the scene yards in front of him. Professor Ziad's pipe fell silently to the damp ground as he stood open-mouthed at a scene straight from Hades. Sir Ranulf grabbed Jonny's shaking hand while Sir Harry and Charlie just stared in wonder.

'Oh, God help us,' Professor Ziad sighed as he fell to his knees and began to pray.

Soon, the noise of the screaming dead visibly weakened the protective shield, as did the howling of the winged black horses with their piercing volcano-red eyes and the repetitive lightning bolts repeatedly smashing into it.

'Jonny, what's the time?' Eddie shouted out, trying hard to be heard above the screams.

'Oh God, I forgot to look,' Jonny replied, running back towards the Nemesis. He picked up the egg timer and noticed that the sand had run out but was unsure exactly when it had run out. Eddie ran over to check the egg timer, grabbing it from Jonny's tiny hands. He swiftly turned it over and watched as the sand began to fall.

'Guess the time, Jonny, just guess the time,' Eddie shouted.

'But how?' Jonny asked, shrugging his shoulders.

'Don't think, just know,' Eddie replied when suddenly a large crack appeared in the protective shield, but unbeknown to all and sundry, the light that now flooded out into the dark sky began to destroy the Outriders from Hell. One by one, as soon as the pure light touched them, they dropped like black rain, smashing to the earth and vaporising as soon as they felt the ground.

Lightning strikes continued to smash into the protective light shield, which resulted in more pure light escaping and destroying the evil Outriders from Hell, who were now falling and vaporising in their hundreds. As soon as one crack appeared, it somehow miraculously repaired itself.

'Wow, that's some protection we have,' Sir Harry quipped.

'No, that's the beings of pure light giving their lives to protect us all,' Jonny replied in awe.

'Quickly, Jonny, you must get ready,' Sir Ranulf said, ushering Jonny, Legion and Legend towards the Nemesis.

'What the hell is that?' Sir Ranulf shouted as he pointed towards the darkened skies. Everyone stopped in their tracks to stare at the sight before them. A huge mass of black cloud encircled the protective shield, and at its heart was a flaming chariot pulled by ten black as-midnight wild stallions with piercing eyes that resembled hot lava dripping from a volcano and there, on the back of the flaming chariot, stood Deadsheda.

'Don't look at her, don't look at her,' Eddie screamed, but it was too late as standing by the kitchen door was Nanny Noo, who was staring directly into the evil face of the devil's only child. Nanny Noo started to vomit; her skin paled as the blood drained from her face.

* * * * * * *

In a flash, Jonny, Legend, and Legion grabbed her and pushed her back into the kitchen just in time before the evil of Deadsheda engulfed her soul. Jonny disappeared to his bedroom and instantly

returned holding two of the life-changing phials.
Jonny held Nanny Noo's head and gently poured
one single drop from each phial into the corner of
Nanny Noo's ashen, trembling mouth.

Eddie rushed in moments later, picking up Nanny
Noo, running straight into the lounge, and gently
placing her in front of the now roaring, angry fire.
Nanny Noo slowly closed her tired eyes as she
began to lose her battle for life.

'Thank you for giving me the happiest years of my
life,' she whispered to Lady Kathleen, grabbing her
delicate hands and adding, 'Now I must go.'

Nanny Noo died in peace alone with her daughter,
Lady Kathleen, who openly wept while caressing
the now smiling, peaceful face of her Mother.

'Oh, Mother, please don't leave me, not now,
please not now,' Lady Kathleen said, her voice
trembling with emotion.

'She has gone,' Sir Ranulf said calmly as he put
his powerful arms around his wife's delicate
shoulders.

Jonny stood open-mouthed with tears streaming
down his red cheeks.

'I thought I could save her; I thought I had the
power to save her. I am a failure,' Jonny said,
crying.

'Jonny, you must go, and you must go now. By my
reckoning, you have almost run out of time,' Eddie
said firmly while gently wiping the tears from
Jonny's face.

* * * * * * *

Jonny ran out of the kitchen door, screaming his
rage towards Deadsheda, who was still circling the

protective shield, laughing maniacally while yelling, 'Death by custard, death by custard.' Jonny stood for a moment as he began to realise what was happening.

This wasn't a dream, this wasn't a game, this was for real, and if he didn't win this battle, it did mean the end of life on earth. Jonny began to weep uncontrollably at the loss of Nanny Noo, the first person to show him love. He remembered his very first day when, after being dropped off at his new home, he first met the kindly older woman and laughed at himself when he remembered falling flat on his face and the conversation that followed. Jonny's heart lightened at the memory of shopping in the quaint town of Little Plopping, where they had shared laughter over the silly name and the bumbling policeman Ivor Ploppy. But now, anger and controlled rage burned in his soul, fuelling his determination to avenge what Deadsheda had taken from him and his family. With Legend and Legion by his side, he felt a newfound strength and assurance. His path was clear, his mind was set, and he was ready to face whatever lay ahead. With a leap, Jonny plunged into Nemesis's vast, echoing depths, stealing one last glance at his home. Eddie and Sir Harry waved, their figures growing smaller as they retreated to the safety of home. The door closed behind him, its soundless click echoing in the silence. He snatched up the egg timer, watching the last grain of sand fall, and quickly flipped it over. As he calculated the time, he realised he had a mere twenty minutes, seventeen of which would be consumed by his journey to Amaranta.

'To Amaranta,' Jonny said out loud. There was no response, nothing.

'Ut Amaranta,' Jonny said again, but this time in Latin.

'Ita, quod nomen est tibi?' (Yes, what is your name?) The computer replied.

Jonny thought for a second as he tried to remember how to speak, let alone understand Latin.

'Ego farcimine, nihil volui, ego have ventus,' (I am a sausage, no I meant, I have wind) Jonny replied having no idea what he was talking about.

'Quod nomen est tibi,' the ship's computer asked again.

'Et est nomen meum imo recto,' (My name is Bottom Burp) Jonny replied.

The computer said, 'Etiam possum credere quod' (yes, I can believe that), began to laugh, and then added, 'Ok laxat.' (OK, let's go).

Within a few seconds, the giant spaceship had turned skywards with astonishing power and unbelievable thrust. Nemesis punched a hole through the protective shield, blinding and destroying many thousands of the Outriders from Hell and many thousands of the beings of pure light, as they filled the gaps left by not only Nemesis but also by repairing the protective shield. Jonny sat in the world's most comfortable seat to contemplate the enormity of what was going on and the ability of so many to give their lives to save just a few.

* * * * * * *

'Hic sumus,' (we're here) said the gentle voice of the computer.

Jonny stood and poured all ten buckets of water into the old tin bath. Placing the hose pipe into the water, he began to blow harder and faster until there were millions of tiny air bubbles. Jonny then checked the egg timer, and again, he caught it just in time as the last grain of sand dropped effortlessly and almost in slow motion.

'Ok, I have seventeen minutes to get in and out,' Jonny muttered under his breath while wiping the beads of sweat from his forehead. Legend and Legion stood beside Jonny, waited for the mini-explosion of light, and prayed. Jonny could remember the words of the Lord's Prayer in Aramaic and what buttons to press while counting down the remaining few minutes.

* * * * * * *

Meanwhile, back on Earth, the protective shield was becoming increasingly weaker. It was as if the Outriders from Hell were allowing themselves to be used like lemmings jumping off a cliff to weaken the shield ultimately. They had little fear of dying as they were already dead and were happy to obey the evil Deadsheda, who had yet to appear; it was as if she was waiting for something or someone.

Soon, more and more Outriders from Hell appeared, swarming around the sky, and anyone foolish enough to be caught outside and unprotected would be sure to meet a very grizzly death, their souls devoured ravenously by the evil devil child. Sadly, for many, this was precisely what was happening.

Millions of people were dying, and Jonny was helpless to change the course of their decisions. Everyone had a choice: leave for safety or perish. Too many chose to stay fearful of losing their money and belongings. In every corner of the world, the Outriders from Hell devoured and destroyed. Many people prayed to God, hoping that they would be saved. Sadly, they hadn't listened to the warnings, and no amount of praying would help. Royalty, politicians, popes and millionaires perished as they hadn't heeded the warnings, and soon, their entire cities would be smashed to the ground by the world's most powerful machine, which had lain hidden for thousands of years.

The machine was built by aliens for this exact moment in time but was built many thousands of years ago and cleverly hidden under the three pyramids of Giza. A machine so powerful it would lay waste to entire countries, killing anyone and anything in its path. Luckily, all this world's animals knew and understood and were safely hidden amongst the thousands of safe caves dotted around the earth. Soon, the body count was in the millions, but the truth was that only the greedy and selfish thought they were better than everyone else suffering.

* * * * * * *

Lady Kathleen ran out of the lounge screaming hysterically and into Sir Ranulf's arms. 'What's the matter, old cabbage?' Sir Ranulf asked gently.

'It's Nanny Noo, its Nanny Noo,' Lady Kathleen repeated, shaking.

'Yes, I know, she has passed away, darling,' Sir Ranulf said reassuringly.

'No, no, I mean Nanny Noo has gone, disappeared into thin air,' Lady Kathleen said as she grabbed Sir Ranulf by his gnarled hands, dragged him into the lounge, and pointed at the sheet in front of the blazing fireplace.

'Good grief,' Sir Ranulf said as he walked over and tentatively removed the white sheet from the floor, adding...' but how and where could she have gone?'

'Come quick, come quick, Deadsheda is, is, is...' Charlie stuttered while grabbing Lady Kathleen and Sir Ranulf. They all rushed outside to be met by Eddie, Mac, over one hundred heavily armed Special Forces soldiers and nearly all the people who were supposed to have stayed hidden in the chalk mines.

Everyone was staring up into the top of the shield. Charlie, Sir Ranulf, and Lady Kathleen looked up to see Deadsheda's vile, contorted face; she was trapped between good and evil. Her vile body writhed as the beings of pure light trapped her; she couldn't move forward, and she couldn't move backwards. She screamed so loud that everyone covered their ears. Some fainted, and some had blood dripping from their ears. Eddie and his hardened regiment ignored the screams and torrents of vile abuse that dripped from the repugnant, foul mouth and aimed enough hardware in her direction to blow her to smithereens.

Suddenly, the night sky was filled with literally thousands of Storm Riders, and at the very same time, Nanny Noo appeared ghost-like, standing by the kitchen door. She looked the same—a tough, no-nonsense woman who had survived two world wars in her lifetime.

'Nanny, Nanny Noo, what are you doing here?' a very shocked Lady Kathleen asked.

'I'm back to fight that evil witch. I may be dead, but I will not rest until I have beaten her and either sent her back to hell where she belongs or destroyed her,' Nanny Noo said, pointing towards Deadsheda.

Suddenly, Nanny Noo flew into the air as Lady Kathleen passed out on the spot.

'Can we not trap her like we did with the Gnud Repeek?' Charlie shouted out to the now floating Nanny Noo.

'No, she must be destroyed,' Nanny Noo replied forcefully.

The Storm Riders encircled the Outriders from Hell and, in a hail of brilliant light, began shooting arrows made of pure light. The Outriders from Hell dropped dead instantly and suddenly changed into angels who then turned on the other Outriders from Hell. The battle between good and evil had begun.

Arrow after arrow of pure light smashed into the evil souls of Deadsheda's army, and one by one, each evil entity was transformed into more beings of pure light. Deadsheda was growing weaker by the minute; her armies of the dead began to fall in their droves. Darkened souls turned into light, and Deadsheda knew she was in trouble.

'Gnud Repeek, where are you?' she screamed, her voice weakening by the second.

Nanny Noo saw this as her opportunity to end the evil reign of the cruel, evil child from hell and, in an instant, flew to where Deadsheda was trapped and struck her. It knocked the tongue-eating parasite clean out of her mouth, which died instantly, shrivelled and screaming.

Nanny Noo took another well-aimed punch, and another, and another. Professor Ziad jumped up and down in pure excitement, shadowboxing Nanny Noo's every move. Nanny Noo hit Deadsheda with a right, left, and then an uppercut, cheered on by everyone gathered below. Deadsheda was spent; she could hardly breathe from the battering she was getting from a frail, very dead, but hard-as-nails Nanny Noo.

* * * * * * *

Jonny was now ready. He had counted down the seventeen minutes to precisely the correct time, and if he hadn't, all would fail, and the evil Deadsheda would take over the earth. He had created millions of bubbles and remembered the exact words of the Lord's Prayer so that he could recite them ideally and in Aramaic.

Jonny began to shout at the top of his voice when suddenly, not just light appeared, but the ring he was carrying from the remains of Dances with Death began to shudder in Jonny's pocket. Jonny quickly removed the bone ring and noticed it had the same triangular shape he once had on his throat.

Suddenly, it began to shine brighter and brighter. Jonny thought momentarily, wondering if this was a good or a bad sign. He stood there for what seemed an eternity, eventually coming to his senses when Legion and Legend reminded him in no uncertain terms to 'pull his finger out.'
Jonny screamed at the bubbles while holding onto the ring of bone. In a flash of brilliant white light, Jonny, Legend and Legion suddenly vanished, only to reappear inside the strangest room he had ever been in, made entirely of mirrors. Jonny opened his palm, and the light from the bone ring shone so bright that it lit up everything as if it were daylight.
Jonny began to recite the Lord's Prayer in Aramaic:
'Aboon dabashmaya
(Our Father in Heaven)
Nethkadash shamak
(Holy is thy name)
Tetha malkoothak
(Your kingdom is coming)
Newe tzevyanak
(Your will be done)
AYKAN DABASHMAYA
(On Earth as it is in heaven)
AF BARA HAV LAN LAKMA DSOONKANAN
(Give us bread for our needs day by day)
Yamana washbook lan
(Forgive us our offences)
KAVINE AIKANA DAF
(As we have forgiven our offenders)
HANAN SHABOOKAN IHAYAVINE OOLOW TALAHN LANESYANA
(Do not let us enter into temptation)

ELA FATSAN MEN BEESHA'

(Deliver us from error).

Quietly, the mirrors covering the four walls, ceiling and floor vanished to reveal the most complicated hieroglyphics Jonny or anyone had ever seen. The entire room was made from solid gold and shone brilliantly. Jonny stood open-mouthed, trying to decipher the thousands of shapes and signs. Suddenly, a small drawer silently fell open to reveal a slight indentation of the same size and triangular shape on the bone ring and Jonny's throat.

'I think the ring goes in there,' Legend said, nudging Jonny.

'Yes, I think you are right,' Jonny replied, placing the bone ring inside the small drawer, which slowly closed.

Then, out of nowhere, a deep, dark voice began to count down.

Yod (10)

Teth (9)

Cheth (8)

Zayin (7)

Vau (6)

Heh (5)

Daleth (4)

Gimel (3)

Beth (2)

Aleph (1)

Abetu yikir Belen (Lord have mercy)

* * * * * * *

Suddenly, the ground began to shake furiously around the bases of all three pyramids. Great chasms opened as the ground thundered like a powerful earthquake. Menkaure began to rise majestically inch by inch, and then Khafre started to move. The shadows of all three pyramids resembled a gigantic intergalactic machine, and they slowly rose into the night sky.

Khufu, the largest of the three pyramids, began to move as the ground around them disappeared into ancient gullies built by aliens many thousands of years ago. The sand that had held the pyramids in place for thousands of years continued to slip effortlessly into the gullies as the counterbalance slowly moved the three giant monoliths into place. Within a few minutes, the three pyramids aligned with the nine planets of our solar system and those of Pashoo.

In all its glory stood the most powerful machine in the universe, The Pulse Detonator, pointing skyward.

* * * * * * *

Jonny stood motionless, fearful of Khufu's noise and slow movement. Legend and Legion stood close to Jonny when a powerful ray of light suddenly lit up an ancient corridor.

Jonny began to run down the corridor with Legend and Legion at his side, and within seconds, he found himself outside the great pyramid between the great feet of the Sphinx. The cold night air made Jonny shiver, but the Nemesis was before him. Jonny quickly jumped into the small opening in the side, followed by Legend and Legion, the doorway silently closing behind them.

'Ok, laxat,' Jonny shouted.

Nemesis turned on its axis, pointed skywards, and effortlessly rose to about one thousand metres into the night sky.

'Vigilate Hoc,' (watch this) the soft voice of the ship's computer said as it opened the transparent floor to reveal a sight that almost made Jonny faint. The three pyramids of Giza were now pointing skywards, an enormous construction of unparalleled power. From nowhere, lightning bolt after a lightning bolt hit the base of the Great Pyramid.

'Quid est quod vocatur?' (What is that called?) Jonny asked, trembling.

'Mortem,' (Death) the computer replied.

Suddenly, an enormous, explosive power pulse erupted into the sky, transforming the night into a blinding, searing light. The earth convulsed as the mighty pulse obliterated everything in its path, reducing it to mere rubble. Any human foolish enough to be caught outside would be annihilated. Pulse after pulse of blinding light erupted, each more astonishing than the last, into the once silent night.

'Redeamus Domum,' (We must return home) Jonny said quietly, almost apologetically. Nemesis turned to the west and, with unearthly power, punched its way home, leaving Mortem to continue destroying the evil that was Deadsheda.

* * * * * * *

'She is mine,' a loud voice echoed. Everybody turned to see Nerrac standing majestically next to Jonny.

'She is mine,' Nerrac repeated.

The vile, bent, stinking body of Deadsheda lay twitching on the ground with one hundred fully loaded guns pointing directly at her. In one swift move, Nerrac ran over to where Deadsheda lay and bit the head of the dying daughter of death clean off, and with his massive claws, ripped open her chest to reveal a slowly beating black heart. He cut the evil black heart into ribbons with a slashing motion of his giant claws.

'You may leave us, Nanny Noo,' Nerrac said in his majestic voice.

Jonny couldn't look up at Nanny Noo's ghost because he knew he was just too late to save her life, and he felt terrible. He began to cry uncontrollably; the past few days had taken their toll on the young boy.

'I am going nowhere, and I am going nowhere fast. I chose to die, Jonny; I chose to die as my days were over and my time had come. I wouldn't leave you or my family without a fight and never leave you. I will live here with my deceased husband, Stan. Do you remember the goolie in the attic, Jonny, who scared Sergeant Flaps? Well, that was my husband, and from now on, I will be back with the love of my life forever.'

The dark clouds in the sky began to disappear as the sun rose.

'Now we wait for Monostomous,' Firestorm said majestically, and immediately from every corner of the sun-kissed sky appeared huge clouds growing larger and larger with every second. Soon, the clouds began to spin slowly, spitting out hailstones the size of cricket balls. As the clouds spun faster and faster, the cricket-sized hailstones were replaced with rain that poured from the heavens in torrents.

The clouds grew darker, and then suddenly, out of the belly of the storm clouds came the most powerful tornadoes anyone had ever witnessed. This was the Monostomous, the million-mouthed destroyer of the evil dead.

One million savage tornadoes hit the earth with shuddering power at the same time, sucking up all the corpses of the evil dead. The wind howled and howled as the tornadoes screamed across the world, removing every remnant of the great battle between good and evil. The wind howled so loudly that the people still safe inside the protective shield ran back to the chalk mines for cover.

Within ten frightening minutes, silence fell on Earth, and the Mortem aimed its last powerful volley into the centre of the world's most giant tornado, completely obliterating it. There was a deathly silence.

The clicking of machine guns being readied to fire broke the eerie silence. The Special Forces soldiers led by Eddie aimed their hardware at the remains of Deadsheda, and the order to open fire was given. In a volley of ear-splitting sounds, the soldiers emptied their full magazines into what remained of Deadsheda, who was then systematically torn to shreds.

Charlie poured some petrol over the still wriggling, oozing, moving body parts of the evil Deadsheda. Eddie took out five large cigars from his shirt pocket and handed one to Sir Ranulf, Sir Harry, Professor Ziad, and Mac. He placed his cigar in the side of his grizzled, weather-beaten, hard-as-nails face and lit his and the other four cigars.

Then, as if in slow motion, he flicked the still burning match towards the still wriggling body parts of Deadsheda, and in one enormous plume of fire and smoke, Deadsheda was no more.
'What happened to the Gnud Repeek?' Lady Kathleen asked quietly.
'After seeing today's battle, he is probably hiding if he was even here,' Eddie said with a resigned, couldn't-care-less sigh. Nerrac morphed back into Legend and Legion, and Jonny silently and slowly slumped to the floor.
* * * * * * *

'Jonny, you need to wake up,' Nanny Carole said in her dark, melted chocolate voice.
Jonny opened his tired eyes to see Nanny Carole standing by the bedroom door, smiling a beautiful, warm, radiant smile. Legend and Legion jumped up onto the bed and licked Jonny awake.
'Wow, now that was what I call a dream,' Jonny said, yawning.
'What dream was that fungus face?' Legend asked.
'Oh, it was all about how I saved the world from the evil Deadsheda,' Jonny replied, stretching his tired body.
'Were we in your dream?' Legion asked.
'Why yes, how did you know that?' Jonny replied with mild surprise.
'Oh, I don't know, perhaps just a lucky guess,' Legend replied.
'I expect you're hungry after all your heroics in your dream?' Nanny Carole asked, smiling.
'Oh, rather, I could eat a horse,' Jonny said, slipping out of his warm bed and into his slippers.

'Sorry, no horses today apart from Firestorm, Starshell, and the Storm Riders,' Nanny Carole said, trying not to giggle.

'Yes, not to mention Cosmos, Spirit, Cheroo, The Beings of Pure Light, Monostomous, Mortem, Nemesis, The Outriders from Hell, Dances with Death, and Deadsheda,' Legion added.

'How on earth did you know that? They were all in my dream,' Jonny said, open-mouthed in surprise.

'Oh, perhaps another lucky guess,' Legend said, nudging Jonny towards the bedroom window.

Jonny rubbed his eyes and took a second and third look. There, below him, were thousands of people, including Eddie and his grinning Special Forces men, Charlie, Sir Ranulf, Lady Kathleen, Sir Harry, Lady Bunty, Professor Ziad, Philomena Flatulent Fudge-Bucket, Dentro Reclu, PC Floppy, and Rabbcat.

'I expect Nanny Noo's making everyone tea,' Jonny said innocently.

'Look again,' Nanny Carole said gently, 'standing next to Lady Kathleen.'

'Oh yeah, but hold on, she doesn't look... no, that's not Nanny Noo,' Jonny stuttered.

Nanny Noo waved, and Jonny waved back, unsure of what was happening. He then began to remember, and he also began to cry.

'Three cheers for Jonny,' Sir Ranulf shouted.

'Hip hip HOORAH, hip hip HOORAH, hip hip HOORAH,' everyone replied in full voice and applauded Jonny.

'You're a hero, Jonny Plumb, and you're my hero,' Nanny Carole said, putting a warm arm around Jonny's shaking shoulders.

'So, my wonderful dream! It wasn't a wonderful dream at all, was it?' Jonny replied, unable to lift his head and look at the crowds of people still applauding him.

'Jonny, you saved the world,' Legend and Legion said in unison.

'Why me, Legend, and why all the pain and suffering?' Jonny asked, wiping the tears from his young face.

'Jonny, pain, grief, loss, ceaseless battles and frustrations of every conceivable kind are there for a real and painfully dramatic reason. We need to wake everybody up and enable us to remove ourselves from ourselves and release what we are truly good at. And Jonny, you happen to be one of the greatest because you know and understand that journey,' Sir Ranulf said, picking Jonny up and hugging him close.

'Come on, some people want to meet you,' Sir Ranulf added. Taking Jonny by his hand, still in his dressing gown and slippers, and holding Pod, they strolled down the staircase to the back garden.

* * * * * * *

Jonny stood silently, his skinny little legs shaking uncontrollably as everyone bowed graciously towards Jonny and again spontaneously began to clap.

'We are free, we are free, we are free,' they all chanted.

'Jonny, you have a few more things to do before this ends. The first is to have a hot bath and go and see Blueshadow, then eat a hearty breakfast, rest, and then have a party.'

Jonny walked over to where Nanny Noo was standing and whispered.

'I'm sorry I didn't get back in time, Nanny Noo, didn't get back in time to save you.'

'My darling child, you got back in time alright, but it was my choice to fly, and I made that choice a long time ago, but don't worry, I'm going nowhere,' Nanny Noo replied, smiling.

'You mean you are going to live with us forever?' Jonny asked.

'Well, as long as you want me and my husband to,' Nanny Noo said, pointing to the almost invisible man in a suit so sharp it had a degree in psychology standing just behind her.

'Husband, Nanny Noo, you have a husband?'

'Who slapped Sergeant wet pants and made that ghostly sound?' Nanny Noo said, smiling. 'Jonny, I want you to meet Stan and Stan, I want you to meet the most wonderful child in the world.'

'Alright, my old son, sorry about me and the trouble (trouble and strife = wife) being brown bread (brown bread = dead) and all that. One day, I'll tell you a jackanory (story) about me and the duchess (Duchess of fife = wife) when we were both on the floor (poor) without two pennies in our skyrockets (pockets). I didn't even own a warm weasel and stoat (coat) or, for that matter, a sharp whistle (whistle and flute = suit) or even a decent dickie dirt (shirt) and had holes in my daisy roots (boots), and if that wasn't bad enough, I also had a bad case of Farmer Giles (piles),' Stan said in his broad cockney accent.

'What did he just say?' Jonny asked, giggling.

'Ok, Jonny, your bath is ready,' Nanny Carole
shouted from Jonny's bedroom window.

* * * * * * *

Jonny gently touched the beautiful turquoise water
of his bath, and in an instant, it heated to just the
right temperature. Jonny slid into the soothing
waters and quietly began to hum when all hell
broke loose as all his sea-life friends emerged
from their hiding places.
'Quickly, Blueshadow wants to see you,' Sloppy
Botty shouted.
Jonny dived deep into the beautiful water to see
Blueshadow sitting beside the pedestal. The
Golden Globe was now back in its rightful home,
shining with renewed beauty, and in Blueshadow's
hand was the Shard of Pure Light.
'Now the war is over,' Blueshadow whispered as
she handed Jonny the Shard of Pure Light.
'All you have to do now is to place it in the earth at
the centre of your back garden, and once that is
done, every shield across the world will be
removed, and every cave entrance will open.'
Jonny tentatively took the Shard of Pure Light
from Blueshadow's delicate hand.
'Thank you, Jonny. You saved our world,'
Blueshadow said quietly as she gently kissed
Jonny on his forehead, and then she vanished
with a swish of her long tail.
Jonny swam to the surface as all the sea life
gathered around him and began to clean him; he
began to sing…

'I fly around the universe

In a spaceship made from light
I travel in the daytime
Then sometimes I fly at night
All around the universe
In a spacecraft made of light
I have been to see the pyramids
In a spaceship made of light
I went there just after teatime
Just when the time was right
I flew to see the pyramids
In a spaceship made from light
I went to see nine angels
In a spaceship made from light
Got to Pashoo at the right time
A most spectacular sight
I went to see nine angels
In a spaceship made from light.

'Well, Jonny, what was saving the world like then?'
Sloppy Botty asked.

'Tiring and incomplete,' Jonny replied, jumping out
of the bath as he realised his work hadn't been
finished yet. First, he had to place the shard of
pure light into the earth and then find Isobel.'

'Yeah, and then rebuild every building, church,
house, and school,' Sloppy Botty added while
letting off a particularly smelly parp.

'No, Sloppy Botty, the third thing I will do is cure
your wind.'

Suddenly, all the sea life began to sing
'You can save the world from evil
Fly invisibly through the skies
You can slay the child of the devil
And cook a half-decent Satan pie
But there is just one thing you cannot do
However hard you try

No amount of sly and cunning
And your God's can't tell you why
Is
Stop a Sloppy Botty
Parping in the sea
Stop a Sloppy Botty
Parping in the sea
You can save the universe from evil
Bring peace and love to our shores
You can slay Deadsheda and the Devil
And make a half decent three witch pie
But there's just one thing you cannot do
No matter how you try
No amount of sly and cunning
And your Gods can't tell you why
Is
Stop a Sloppy Botty
Parping in the sea
Stop a Sloppy Botty
Parping in the sea.'

* * * * * * *

Jonny stood by the kitchen door with Legend and Legion by his side. The garden had been cleared and almost returned to its immaculate best, and everyone had gathered and formed a giant semi-circle. Jonny scanned all the faces staring back at him and felt sad when he saw Nanny Noo looking tearful and Rabbcat rubbing against her ghost legs, but even more tragic when he couldn't see Isobel. Jonny slowly walked towards the centre of the semi-circle in absolute silence. He knelt on one knee and placed the shard of pure light into the ground, and as he did, ripple after ripple, wave after wave of pure light, radiated outwards, filling everybody with a feeling of heavenly rapture. Some fell to their knees ecstatically, some cried out loud, while others just smiled with happiness and contentment. Soon, the ripples of pure light contacted the protective shield. In one incredible jaw-dropping explosion of brilliant white light, it disappeared along with every other shield of pure light protecting other buildings and people worldwide.

A deathly silence seemed to hang in the air for ages, followed by a morning chorus of thousands of birds singing happily and free. Then, slowly and tentatively, all the world's animals emerged from the many secluded, safe caves and havens dotted around the earth to a new world of freedom.

Jonny removed the shard of pure light as the most beautiful day on earth began.

Legend and Legion's ears pricked up, turning their massive heads towards the house and then looking up towards the roof, sniffing the air.

'What is it?' Jonny asked.

But before he got a reply, Legend and Legion had run back towards the house. Within a few seconds, they had climbed the stairs and sat whining while looking up at the closed attic door. Jonny stood next to them when they heard a knock, knock, knock, followed by a very frightened little voice.

'Help, help me, please help me.'

'Oh my God, it's Isobel,' Jonny shouted, jumping up and down joyfully. Knowing the metal rod to the latch in the attic was broken, he took one giant leap and dragged the attic hatch open. There stood Isobel, shivering and covered in custard.

Jonny ran up the few wooden, creaking stairs and hugged Isobel with all his might. Then, he picked her up and carried her down the creaking old stairs into the bathroom, where he ran a lovely bath for her. Since there was still no gas, he gently tested the beautiful turquoise water, which instantly became piping hot. Jonny picked up Isobel, still covered from head to toe and trembling with cold, and gently placed her in the bath.

'What on earth happened?' Jonny asked as Legend and Legion stood guard.

Isobel tried to speak, but there was no sound. Jonny leaned forward to hear what she was saying when Isobel softly whispered...

'I love you, Jonny.'

The life-giving and cleansing waters of Jonny's bath began to work their magic as Sir Ranulf and Lady Kathleen soon arrived with nice, warm, dry towels.

'Quickly, tell Charlie to get the fire going and ask Nanny Carole to make some food, but it is probably best not to make custard. Oh, and get her some of my clothes,' Lady Kathleen instructed Sir Ranulf.

* * * * * * *

Jonny, Legend, and Legion waited patiently in the lounge for Isobel to finish her bath. The fire roared, happy and bright. Nanny Carole brought in some bread and gently heated it until it was light brown and hot, placing a skewer through the centre of each slice. Jonny quickly spread some margarine and marmalade and went to take a bite, but it was swiftly taken away from him by a smiling

Isobel, who was now dressed head to toe in Lady Kathleen's finest clothes. Her hair shone and reflected the light of the fire.

'So, how are you feeling now, custard breath?' Jonny asked, laughing.

'Oh, ha ha,' Isobel replied, eating slice after slice of the warm toast.

'So, what did happen?' Sir Ranulf asked as they were soon joined by Sir Harry, Lady Pinner, Professor Ziad, and Philomena.

'Oh God, it was horrible. I was in the car with my mother when we were stopped by a fallen tree, and out of nowhere, this ugly witch on a broom grabbed hold of me and flew straight into your attic via the skylight.'

'What happened to your mother?' Lady Kathleen asked.

'Probably too heavy to fit on the broom,' Jonny laughed.

'She ran away, ran for her life, but I don't know where. Is she not here?' Isobel asked.

'No, no one has seen her or your father. They weren't in the chalk mines, and if they weren't in the chalk mines...' Jonny stopped for a second, not wanting to tell Isobel what had probably happened, but he knew he had to. 'Well, they wouldn't have survived unless they found somewhere underground to hide. So, let's not give up hope yet.'

'I'll get Eddie and his men to search the area,' Sir Ranulf said, but before he could stand and go talk to Eddie, there was a 'knock, knock' on the front door.

'I'll get it,' Charlie said, walking out of the enormous oak doors and into the hall.

'Guess who it was?' Charlie said, smiling.
Everybody turned to see that Big Chief Runny
Stool and Laughs with Parps were holding the
hands of Isobel's parents, who were in tears.
'Mummy, Daddy!' Isobel shouted and jumped up
to hug her rather tired and dirty-looking parents.
'We thought we had lost you, lost you forever,'
Isobel's mother and father said as they both fell to
their knees, sobbing uncontrollably.
'I was wrong about what I said about you, Jonny,
so wrong,' Isobel's mother said as she dried the
remaining tears of joy from her eyes and then
added, 'Thank you, thank you so much for saving
our beautiful child's life.'
'Aw shucks, it was nothing,' Jonny replied, smiling.
'So, what happened then? What did we miss?'
Isobel's mother asked.
'Oh, not much,' Lady Kathleen said, smiling.
'Well, let's begin with Isobel's story as none of us
know what happened there,' Lady Kathleen said,
but before she could tell her story, the ghost of
Nanny Noo and Stan brushed past Isobel's
mother, who promptly shrieked and passed out.
'Whoops,' Nanny Noo said, giggling as she and
Stan sat down next to Jonny while Lady Kathleen
gently woke Isobel's mother.
'G-G-Ger Ghost!' Isobel's mother said, pointing at
Nanny Noo and Stan.
'Yes, G-G-Ger Ghosts,' Nanny Noo and Stan
replied, then went for a quick fly around the
lounge, making everybody laugh.
'So, come on, old girl, how did you survive?' Sir
Ranulf asked Isobel impatiently.
'Well, once we got into the attic, Dances with
Death tied me up and said she would let me go if I

told her where the one hundred phials were hidden. But I knew she was lying, so I kept quiet. Then she began to get angrier and angrier, making her uglier. And then I saw that Dances with Death was three hags in one ugly witch. I was petrified, but I wasn't going to tell them anything. Then she put a vile-smelling piece of cloth into my mouth, blindfolded me, and tied my hands up. Then she put me in the darkest part of the attic, and then, I heard you, Jonny, with Legend and Legion. I could listen to you, but I couldn't see you. I tried to scream, but the dirty rag in my mouth made it impossible. Then she started to float in the air, rocking to and fro, and I felt sick. I'm sick of her vile smell and the rocking. But as soon as she heard the word 'custard,' I knew instinctively that you had her beaten.'

'So, are you trying to tell us that after we killed her, we couldn't see you because of the dirty old rags and the custard?' Jonny asked.

'Yes, yes. I was trying to shout, but I still had the dirty old rag in my mouth. Bit by bit, I managed to spit it out, but then you left, and I thought I was going to die. I was so cold and so frightened of the noises coming from outside. The thunder and lightning made me so scared, alone in the pitch dark. I thought you had left me, and I was going to die,' Isobel started to cry uncontrollably and then added, 'I never want to see, smell or taste custard for the rest of my life.'

Jonny put his arm around Isobel's trembling shoulders and felt something wasn't right.

'What's the matter?' Jonny asked quietly.

'There was something in the attic with me,' Isobel replied, still shaking, and in a flash, Eddie and a few of his heavily armed men ran up the stairs and into the attic.

'Nothing there now,' Eddie said, walking calmly into the lounge.

'Oh, but there was, and I heard it,' Isobel replied, still shaking.

'What do you mean? What was there?' Jonny asked.

'I don't know, as I couldn't see it, but I could hear it breathing and smell it. Eugh, it was revolting. I just kept still, and when you had killed Dances with Death, it sounded like it was crying, and then it started to thrash about. I was petrified. I have never been so scared. Then a few hours went by, and I heard it flapping its wings, and then I heard its claws scratching on the walls as it climbed out of the skylight, and then it flew away.'

'Well, that must have been after the shield had come down, as it couldn't have escaped before that,' Sir Ranulf said as Nanny Carole gave Isobel a cold drink of orange juice.

'I still didn't know if I was alone, but I was so petrified I had to call out, and I'm glad I did,' Isobel said, hugging both Legend and Legion.

'So the question is... what on earth was it?' Lady Kathleen asked nervously.

'I also found this,' Isobel said, handing over a very ancient-looking, quite large, leather wallet covered in cobwebs and dust, with strange hieroglyphics written across it. Jonny picked it up and gently opened the almost paper-thin leather to reveal a smaller leather pouch. Jonny carefully opened it, and everyone watched his every move. Jonny pulled out what appeared to be an ancient map.

He placed the map before the roaring fire as everyone sat silently on this weird map.

'What is it, and what does it say?' Professor Ziad asked, craning his neck over the others' heads.

'I have no idea,' Jonny replied.

'It's not like the writing we saw at the Pyramids, right?' Sir Ranulf said, scratching his few days of unshaven stubble on his lantern jaw.

'Stop scratching, darling, you sound like you have fleas,' Lady Kathleen said, laughing.

'Why is it all blurred?' Charlie asked.

'Oh, I know, it's in three dimensions,' Jonny replied and added, 'What we need is a blue lens and a red lens and some plastic.'

Quick as a flash, Professor Ziad had found a blue and red felt-tip pen and an old bit of plastic and drew two lens shapes straight onto the plastic.

'WowWee,' Professor shouted as he stared at the ancient map.

'Quickly, show me,' Sir Ranulf said, grabbing the bit of plastic out of Professor Ziad's hands.

'Cor blimey,' he shouted, and then Lady Kathleen grabbed the plastic, homemade glasses out of Sir Ranulf's hands, peered at the map, and instantly passed out.

Jonny peered excitedly through the red and blue-painted plastic sheet, and what stood out in perfect three dimensions was the most astonishing thing he had ever seen.

Prometheus

CHAPTER TWO:
HIDDEN DANGERS

Jonny lay on his bed staring at the ceiling as Legend and Legion lay beside him.

'So, Jonny, what was the bone ring? How did you know about the bone ring? How did you know the bone ring would fit into that giant computer? What flew out of the attic, and what was that map thing?' Legend asked quietly.

Jonny continued to stare at the ceiling, saying nothing.

'Jonny, didn't you hear me?' Legend asked as he stood up, placing his giant head onto Jonny's chest.

'Yes, I did, Legend, but something just occurred to me, apart from the twenty questions about the bone ring, which, to be honest, I am unsure of,' Jonny replied quietly.

'What's just occurred, Jonny?' Legion asked as he gently stood up, yawning, stretching his muscular body, and shaking so hard that he nearly fell over.

'That the Devil only sent his daughter. I mean, why would the Devil send his only daughter who, let's be honest here, was a bit useless? Not to mention Dances with Death, three all-singing, all-dancing, all-evil, and all-powerful witches from hell who got...'

'...Killed by custard,' Legion and Legend replied in unison.

'Yeah, death by custard,' Jonny said, smiling, and then he started to laugh, soon joined by Legend and Legion.

'Death by custard, death by custard,' they all
shouted.
'Also,' Jonny said, almost whispering, as he gently
stroked Legend's and Legion's massive heads.
'Also, what?' Legend asked, scratching his ear.
'Also, why did Nanny Noo have to die to save us
when it was my job and only my job to kill
Deadsheda? I think there is more trouble to come,'
Jonny sighed.
'There are so many unanswered questions right
now, Jonny,' Sir Ranulf said as he opened Jonny's
bedroom door, 'but right now we have work to do.'

* * * * * * *

Jonny jumped out of bed and quickly got dressed,
stopping to throw some cold water in the general
direction of his face. Then he ran down the two
flights of stairs, where the almost forgotten smell
of cooked food was hanging in the air.
'Sit down, Jonny, and eat up,' Nanny Carole said
in her melted chocolate voice.
'When did we get electricity and gas back?' Jonny
asked while demolishing his first hot breakfast in
ages.
'Oh, the army lads got that sorted. All the supplies
are back to normal, and many people are quietly
rebuilding their lives,' Sir Ranulf replied.

* * * * * * *

Jonny breathed in the fresh morning air while
looking at the beautiful garden, where the birds
sang and squirrels happily chased each other.

'Another new day in paradise,' Charlie said while looking up from tending the garden.

'Yes, it certainly is paradise,' Jonny replied, smiling.

The enormous shield protecting Jonny's home had now gone, and the shard of pure light was once again hidden back where it belonged with the Golden Globe.

Jonny smiled as he sat under his favourite tree with his two faithful companions, Legion and Legend, and whispered.

'We have a lot of work to do.'

'Jonny, do you think the thing we don't know about what flew out of the attic was the Devil?' Legend asked as he sprawled his giant body across the luscious green grass.

'Right now, I know so little that I am surprised I can ever stand upright,' Jonny replied, laughing, 'but I somehow doubt it. I mean, why would he allow his daughter to die? No, I think that something that we don't know is, in fact, something we don't know about. So, therefore, we shouldn't concern ourselves too much over what we don't know.'

'Well, that was about as clear as mud,' Legend replied, wagging his tail furiously as Sir Ranulf arrived.

'Ok, Jonny, we have to go now,' Sir Ranulf said solemnly.

'Go where?' Jonny asked without even opening his eyes.

'Nanny Noo's funeral is today, Jonny, or had you forgotten?'

'Forgotten,' Jonny replied as he vanished into mid-air and returned within a blink of an eye dressed perfectly in his dark suit.

* * * * * * *

The small church of Little Plopping was adorned with every conceivable type of flower, which hung gently in the morning breeze on a lazy Sunday. Windows and doors were draped with some of the world's most beautiful and rare orchids, and the scent was heavenly.

There was absolute silence as Sir Ranulf opened the passenger door of his gleaming Rolls Royce to let out Lady Kathleen, who was soon followed by Nanny Carole, Charlie, and Jonny. Behind them, a steady stream of Nanny Noo's friends, including Sir Harry and Lady Pinner, Professor Ziad and the remarkably silent Philomena Flatulent Fudge-Bucket, Legend and Legion, and behind them, what appeared to be everyone else in the country, had come to pay their final respects to the brave woman who gave her life so others could live.

The church was full to bursting; every seat was taken, and every spare inch was filled with some standing, head bowed in respect. At a given signal by the Vicar, Father William Warmer, or Willie to his closest friends and colleagues, everyone sat down silently, not a word spoken, not even a mistimed cough or loose parp. There, at the front of the packed congregation, stood Nanny Noo's coffin draped with yet more flowers from every corner of the country. Jonny sat down alongside his mother and father on the front bench, heads bowed when Jonny started to giggle.

'Don't cry, darling,' Lady Kathleen said as she put a gentle, caring arm around Jonny's shaking shoulders.

'I, I'm, I'm...' Jonny tried to speak.

'It's ok, Jonny, I know how much you missed Nanny Noo, we all do, darling, we all do,' interrupted Lady Kathleen.

Sadly, Jonny couldn't stop giggling; he giggled so much his eyes were crying from laughter. Jonny nudged Lady Kathleen and whispered...

'Look, look behind Nanny Noo's coffin.' Lady Kathleen looked up, wiping the tears from her eyes, and noticed what Jonny had seen. She began to giggle as well.

'Darling, this isn't an appropriate time to start giggling, darling, is it?' Sir Ranulf whispered to the now almost doubled-in-two Lady Kathleen. Soon, more and more, the once silent congregation started to giggle quietly at first and then louder and louder. Father William Warmer stood perplexed and coughed a couple of times in the hope of restoring some sanity and order. Sadly, Father William Warmer couldn't see what was behind his back, but everybody else could. He then began to speak to the massed congregation.

'We are all gathered here today to remember the life and times of one Nanny Noo...' But before he could utter another word, the congregation fell into hysterics. Father William Warmer was not amused, seeing this as disrespectful behaviour towards the deceased. However, what he failed to see—and what Jonny, Lady Kathleen, and the gathered masses saw—was the ghost of Nanny Noo performing the balloon dance, stark naked. At the same time, her deceased husband played the organ, also stark naked, hiding his modesty behind just a pair of red balloons.

The congregation erupted with laughter, and the small church grew increasingly cramped as people outside vied to get in, having heard the sounds of laughter instead of morbid crying. Father William Warmer never really had a great sense of humour and didn't take kindly to practical jokes of any kind. This made Nanny Noo's last appearance on Earth even funnier, and so far, he couldn't see and had absolutely no idea what everybody else was laughing about.

Jonny almost collapsed on the floor in hysterics as Nanny Noo quickly moved the three strategically placed balloons from one place to another. At the same time, Father William Warmer got angrier and angrier.

'We are all gathered here today,' Father William Warmer started again, but this time almost shouting at the top of his voice. Still, no one noticed as Nanny Noo carried out her last-ever balloon dance. Then, her husband joined her, and together, they performed the funniest balloon dance as the congregation clapped in unison. Nanny Noo and her husband took a long bow and smiled childishly. Jonny's heart began to sink as he realised it was over. Silently, Nanny Noo blew Jonny a kiss, lay on top of her beautiful flower-covered coffin, and slowly disappeared. The clapping ceased, and Jonny wiped the tears of laughter away as tears of utter heartbreak rolled down his still-pristine cheeks.

Jonny stood up and walked over to the coffin, which held his best, closest, and dearest friend in the whole wide world, the woman he remembers with such love who was there to greet him on his first lonely and frightened day away from his cold, empty orphanage. Nanny Noo showed Jonny not only that he was loved but also that he could show love back. Jonny stood silently, just remembering the happy times and then, without prior warning, began to sing:

When the fields are lush and golden
And the skies are forever blue
When the snowflakes fall in silence
And the raindrops dance, too
I'll be thinking about you, Nanny Noo
About you, Nanny Noo, about you
When I laugh out loud for no reason
As children tend to do
When I'm feeling kind of down and sad
With my head is full of full
I'll remember all about you, Nanny Noo
Remember all about you, Nanny Noo
When I'm tired and hungry
Suffering from nightmares, too
When I toss, I turn, and I fail to go to sleep
I know just what I can do
I will dream of you, Nanny Noo
Dream about you, Nanny Noo
Now, the longest day is over
And the night is almost through
I will sit down and pray for you
Pray for you is what I'll do
I'll pray for your peace and happiness
Just for you, Nanny Noo
Just for you, Nanny Noo, just for you
Jonny placed a lovely white rose on Nanny Noo's coffin.

'Thank you,' Nanny Noo said quietly as Jonny returned to his seat, buried his tearful head in his hands, and wept.

'Please be upstanding for Nanny Noo's favourite song, "Abide with Me."' The congregation stood as one and sang in a great voice.

Lady Kathleen then walked up to Nanny Noo's coffin and, as Jonny had done before, placed a single white rose next to Jonny's.

'Thank you,' Nanny Noo whispered.

Lady Kathleen stood silently for a few seconds, staring at the coffin, before turning to address the congregation with her handwritten eulogy.

'My mother,' Lady Kathleen said, almost whispering. Jonny turned to Sir Ranulf and mouthed, 'Mother?'

'Yes, son, mother,' Sir Ranulf whispered back, then added, 'Now listen.'

'My mother, yes, my mother. I know this will shock everyone here, mainly because she didn't want anyone to know, but now the story can be told: a story of immense bravery and unparalleled courage.'

Lady Kathleen stood upright, rested her left hand gently against the pure white coffin, perhaps for reassurance or to feel closer to her mother, and began to tell her story.

'My mother was cycling home one day after a particularly bad day at the hospital where she worked caring for injured soldiers of the First World War.

One evening, when I was just a few days old, the house where I lived with my birth mother and father was hit by a bomb, killing everyone. Well, everyone except me, as I was thrown under the bath by the force of the bomb. I stayed there for hours, crying and in great fear. While cycling home, Nanny Noo heard my cries and bravely walked inside the now-wrecked house. Next to where I was lying was an unexploded bomb that stopped ticking the moment Nanny Noo found me. She had no idea if the bomb was about to explode or not, but refusing to leave me, she clambered over the rubble, leaking water, gas pipes, and naked flames that could have ignited the leaking gas at any moment. Heroically, Nanny Noo searched the wreckage in total darkness, listening intently to my cries. To keep my attention, she sang a beautiful song, a song I shall never forget, and that song was called "How Deep is the Ocean."' Lady Kathleen began to sing this song, and everyone was astonished at how beautifully she sang.

Lady Kathleen continued her story to a silent and enthralled audience, explaining with pride how 'Nanny Noo managed to move the heavy bath all on her own and just got clear of the house before the enormous bomb blew half the street to smithereens. Severely burnt, lacerated with flying glass, and cut and bleeding badly, Nanny Noo carried me to her home some three miles away. Alone and in great pain, she tended to her appalling injuries without any painkillers. By chance, a policeman who was checking that everyone had turned out their lights heard Nanny Noo sobbing from the pain of her injuries and then noticed me, partly hidden in a mass of rags, in her arms.

The policeman ran the three miles to the hospital to gather more bandages and stole, yes, stole, a bottle of milk, then ran back through the battle-scarred streets and bomb craters, unsure if there were any more unexploded bombs about to detonate. He returned just in time to find Nanny Noo passed out on the floor from loss of blood. He stopped the flow of blood, bandaged her injuries, and covered her with a blanket to warm her now-shaking body. The alarm sounded, and a policeman was seen stealing the small milk bottle he stole to feed me. He was subsequently fired from the police force with a dishonourable discharge. Nanny Noo fell in love with that brave policeman, whose name was Stan, and without telling a soul, they pretended that I was their child and brought me up as their own. Today is the first time this story has been told. They gave up their lives so I could live and never told a single person. Today, we commemorate the unbelievable strength and courage of Nanny Noo.'

Lady Kathleen dabbed the tears that flowed freely down her pristine red cheeks, then hugged Sir Ranulf and Jonny in silence as the entire congregation applauded as one.

Sir Ranulf, Sir Harry, Professor Ziad, and Sergeant Edward Stone marched towards Nanny Noo's coffin. In silence, each man stood to attention and slowly and effortlessly raised the oak coffin shoulder-high, festooned with colours. They walked slowly, heads held high, back through the church and into the most beautiful sunny days. Momentarily, the birds stopped singing as if they were also paying homage to this wonderful person.

Slowly, bit by bit, Nanny Noo's coffin was lowered into her final resting place next to her beloved husband, Stan, as Father William Warmer recited the Lord's Prayer.

Jonny picked up a handful of the warm earth and gently sprinkled it over Nanny Noo's coffin as tears fell freely from his face. Soon, Sir Ranulf, Sir Harry, Professor Ziad, Lady Kathleen, Lady Bunty and Nanny Carole, who were almost unable to stand from grief and were gently helped by Charlie, also threw a small handful of dirt onto the top of the coffin. Soon, everybody who had attended the funeral had, in total silence, added just one handful of dirt.

Jonny walked home with Lady Kathleen, Legend and Legion and was told the entire story of Nanny Noo's life.

'She died to save my life,' Jonny whimpered.

'No, Jonny, she died to save all our lives,' Lady Kathleen whispered.

* * * * * * *

Soon, they had arrived home, and as Jonny looked towards the large oak front doors, he smiled the biggest smile in the world. Standing there, as she had on Jonny's first day, was Nanny Noo, and next to her, Stan, her husband.

'We may have passed on, Jonny, but we will never leave our family,' Nanny Noo whispered as she hugged Jonny and Lady Kathleen.

'We have our very own ghosts,' Jonny said, smiling, reassured that although Nanny Noo had passed away physically, she would always be with them in spirit form.

'I'll make us all a nice cup of tea,' Nanny Noo said reassuringly as Sir Ranulf closed the enormous oak doors.

* * * * * * *

Jonny lay back under his favourite oak tree and began to cry when the ghost of Nanny Noo came and sat down next to him. Legend and Legion rolled on their backs, smiling happily.

'Don't be sad, Jonny; it was my time to go. Legend and Legion are not sad, are they? They understand, Jonny, that we all, even you, will one day pass into the spirit world where you will wait to be reborn to a new life on earth.'

'I know, Nanny, but does that mean that one day you and Stan will also go to the spirit world?' Jonny asked, trying to hold Nanny Noo's almost invisible hand.

'Jonny, we chose to stay here with you and our daughter for a while longer. When you have spent as much time as Stan and I have, caring for your mother, our daughter, and then caring for you, it's not easy to leave you all, but yes, Jonny, one day we will fly.'

Jonny felt tears welling in his eyes again, but he knew he had to be brave for himself and his mother.

* * * * * * *

Big Chief Running Stool and Laughs with Parps floated, still cross-legged, into the lounge where Jonny sat comforting his mother.

'We have a story about the bone ring and the hidden map,' Laughs with Parps whispered.

'How did you know we had found a map?' Jonny asked in mild surprise.

'We have forgotten more than you know,' Laughs with Parps replied, smiling.

'Doesn't your father ever talk?' Lady Kathleen asked.

'Talk? He never stops talking, but you cannot hear him as he only talks with his mind. However, there has been the odd occasion when he uttered a few choice words.'

'So, what is he saying then?' Legend asked as he carefully walked around the hovering Chief.

'Well, if you must ask,' Laughs with Parps replied.

'I must, I must,' Legend said, momentarily stopping to smell Big Chief Running Stool's head.

'Well, if you're sure, I mean, he does go on and on,' Laughs with Parps said while making the sign of a talkative bird with her right hand.

There was a deep, snoring noise as Legion had already fallen fast asleep from boredom.

'So, let me get this right, he never sleeps, stands, walks, eats, washes, sings, talks or plays rugby?' Jonny said, laughing.

'Correct. He doesn't sleep, walk, eat, wash, sing, talk, play rugby, ride a horse, drink water, go to the toilet, make his bed, smoke a peace pipe, say "heap big fat man" or parp. Oh, sorry, he does parp and, man, he parps very quietly, so you don't know, well, apart from the smell and the smoke.'

'What? When he parps, smoke comes out of his butt?' Lady Kathleen asked, unbelieving of what she was being told.

'Yep, sure does; it comes straight out of his butt and ears,' Laughs Parps replied matter-of-factly.

'I don't belie...' but before Lady Kathleen could finish her sentence, Big Chief Running Stool let rip when he instantly went from nought miles per hour to about sixty, just stopping before he crashed into the lounge ceiling.

'Oh my God, that sounded like a plane crashing into the side of a mountain,' Legion said, shaking his tired head.

'You said he didn't make a sound,' Jonny said, holding his nose.

'OK, I admit he sometimes makes the sound of a plane crashing into the side of a mountain,' Laughs with Parps replied, laughing.

'I feel sick,' Lady Kathleen said, opening the lounge windows.

'So do I,' Jonny replied, pretending to pull a toilet chain while holding his nose, then adding.

'Can't you stop him? He has more methane inside of him than Jupiter and could blow up any minute.'

'Can't you put him in a box or something?' Lady Kathleen asked, gasping for fresh air.

Laughs with Parps then floated out of the lounge and into the back garden, quickly followed by Big Chief Bottom Burp, as Jonny had renamed him, and both vanished into thin air.

'Hold on, you were about to tell us about the bone ring and the, err the err, map,' Jonny shouted.

'I will, another time,' Laughs with Parps replied from nowhere.

* * * * * * *

Jonny ran a nice hot bath and was quietly pleased that the once multi-coloured water had reverted to its usual colour. The old water heater chugged and chugged, spewing out gallons of piping hot water, and in one well-practised leap, Jonny was in and immediately surrounded by all his sea life friends.

'OK, Jonny, for the last time, will you tell us all about Buddha?' Sloppy Botty asked impatiently.

'Buddha? What's Buddha?' Jonny replied, laughing.

'It's stuff you put on your toast,' Wall-Eyed Wally replied while he began to wash Jonny's hair, even though Jonny didn't want a face, nose, ear and mouth full of shampoo.

'No, that's butter,' Stench replied.

'What's better?' Sloppy Botty asked.

'Well, not your hearing,' Jonny said, trying to stop Wall-Eyed Wally from emptying all the shampoo onto Jonny's head.

'What's a herring got to do with butter?' Stench asked, all confused.

'No, hearing, not herring. I have never heard of a herring aid or a deaf person with bad herring,' Jonny replied while wiping away the vast amounts of soap from his head.

'What's Sloppy Botty talking about, Jonny?' Harpoon whispered.

'Well, I think he's trying to ask about Bodha, but you know Sloppy, very easily confused.'

'That's what I said, I said, Budgie,' Sloppy Botty shouted while leaping in and out of the soapy bath water.

'No, you said Budgie, silly,' everyone replied unison.

'There is no planet that orbits Pashoo called Budgie, Sloppy Botty. I don't know of any planet in the known universe named after a bird, especially a planet named after a songbird called a Budgie,' Jonny replied, still trying to stop Wall-Eyed Wally from washing his hair.

'Boggy, Badger, Bogie, Bodge, Bridge, and Bandy the Budgie are all planets,' Sloppy Botty shouted as he dived in and out faster and faster.

'He means planet Bodha, the planet of knowledge,' Jonny said, smiling. 'Someone should send him there and soon,' Stench shouted.

'Ok, ok, I will tell you all about the nine orbiting planets if Wall-Eyed Wally stops cleaning my hair and Sloppy Botty stops talking. Is that a deal?'

'YES,' everyone replied.

'Phew, at last,' Jonny sighed.

'Ok, the nine orbiting planets of Pashoo are Bodha, the planet of knowledge where we will send Sloppy Botty, and then there's Boddhi, the planet of enlightenment. Suddha, the planet of purity. Jala, the planet of pure water. Turya, the planet of deep sleep. Krodha, the planet of anger. Yajna, the planet of sacrifice. Mithya, the planet of the unreal, and Tattvam, the planet of reality. Sadly, to Jonny's annoyance, everybody had fallen fast asleep from sheer boredom.

'We're only joking,' Sloppy Botty shouted as the sea life gathered around.

'So, Bodha was the very first planet I went to. I do not know how I arrived, but it was warm, sunny, and beautiful. Every day, I would have to sit in front of a master who just told me information about everything.'

'Such as?' Sloppy Botty asked.

'Ok, well, our galaxy, the Milky Way, is spinning at a rate of two hundred and twenty-five kilometres per second. In addition, the galaxy travels through space at a rate of three hundred kilometres per second. That means we are travelling at a total speed of five hundred and thirty kilometres per second. So, in just one minute, you have moved nineteen thousand kilometres.'

'Zzzzzzzzzzzz,' the sea life all snored at once.

'Well, that was fascinating, Jonny,' Wall-Eyed Wally said, yawning.

'Ok, this is fascinating; did you know your body is billions of years old?' Jonny said, trying to wake his very disinterested audience.

'What are you saying, Jonny, that I'm older than the Earth? I know I am no oil painting, but older than the Earth, I don't think so,' a quite angry Porka the Orca said while nudging Jonny's leg.

'No, listen. Hydrogen, which is, as you know, the most common element in the universe and a major part of all our bodies, was produced in the Big Bang thirteen billion years ago.'

'What Big Bang? I never heard a Big Bang. Did anyone here hear a Big Bang?' Sloppy Botty asked.

'Jonny, this is painfully dull; can't you tell us something interesting?' Stench asked politely.

'Ok, your sense of smell is around ten thousand times more sensitive than your sense of taste,' Jonny said excitedly.

'How about my sense of boredom, which has reached an all-time low, and how long did they teach you all these boring, boring, boring facts?' Porka asked.

'Oh, ten years,' Jonny replied.

'Ok, so let's move on to the next place you visited,'
Stench asked.
'It better be more interesting than the last place,
the planet Bandy Bogie,' Sloppy Botty said while
blowing bubbles from his air hole.
Suddenly, the conversation stopped as Nanny
Carole called Jonny down for dinner.
'Right, gotta go,' Jonny said as he leapt out of the
bath, got dressed, and then ran down the two
flights of stairs and straight into the kitchen, where
a beautiful smell of cooked dinner greeted him.

* * * * * * *

'Laughs with Parps and Big Chief Running Stool
want to talk with you after dinner,' Nanny Carole
said while washing the dishes.
'What about?' Lady Kathleen enquired.
'Unsure, they didn't say... but I think it's something
to do with the hidden map,' Nanny Carole replied
while Jonny stuffed his face with sausages, mash,
and baked beans in silence.
'Ooooo, hidden map, how exciting! Can we
come?' Lady Kathleen asked.
'Well, I don't know where it is yet, but when I do,
yes, why not,' Jonny replied, demolishing his
dinner in seconds flat, adding, 'That was yummy.'

* * * * * * *

Jonny meandered into the garden with Legend
and Legion, where Laughs with Parps hovered
alongside Chief Running Stool and sat down.

'So, what's with this map then?' Jonny asked if, by magic, Big Chief Running Stool produced the old, weather-beaten, torn, strange-looking map from seemingly nowhere.

'OK, first you have to go to a place in Devon called Lyford Gorge,' Laughs with Parps said as she pointed to the map, 'and while you are there, you must find the entrance to a secret cave. You must find a scroll in that secret cave with magic words written down.'

'Easy peasy lemon squeezy,' Jonny said, butting in.

'That is written in Icelandic. You then have to translate the words while you travel to...'

'Iceland?' Legend said nonchalantly while chewing a well-gnawed bone.

'Oooooooooh, clever you, Legend,' Legion said, yawning.

'Yes, as I was saying, travel to Iceland, where you have to find the Ice Queen of Iceland and sing this song to her in Icelandic and then in English.'

'So, OK, seems easy, but where do I find the Ice Queen of Iceland?' Jonny asked.

'Ah, well, that's not too easy as no one has ever seen her,' Laughs with Parps replied coyly, as Big Chief Running Stool smiled.

'Well, if no one has ever seen her, how does anyone know for sure she actually exists?' Legion asked, trying to be as clever as Legend.

'Legend,' Laughs with Parps replied.

'Yes?' Legend replied.

'No, not you, Legend, legend,' Jonny said, smiling.

'She, the Ice Queen of Iceland, lives in the underworld and is protected by everything you could imagine,' Laughs with Parps added while trying to make it sound all scary and failing miserably.

'Such as?' Jonny asked while stroking Legion's massive head.

'Oh, you don't want to know,' Laughs with Parps said, but with real fear in her voice this time.

'Oh yes, I do,' Jonny replied cheekily.

'Oh, no, you don't, really, you don't,' Laughs with Parps added.

'Yes, I do,' Jonny replied, just to annoy Laughs with Parps.

'Err, no, you don't,' came the short, angry reply.

Suddenly, the silly argument stopped when Big Chief Running Stool let off a parp so powerful that he flew two hundred feet straight into the evening sky and straight down again to hover gently without batting an eyelid.

'Why, how, what's wrong with him?' Legend asked while sniffing around the deadly silent Chief.

'Search me,' Laughs with Parps replied, shrugging her shoulders. 'Perhaps it's a clue.'

'Perhaps he's just barking mad,' Legion whispered to Legend.

'A clue? What sort of clue is that? Breaking wind with the power of a Mars-bound rocket, flying two hundred feet into the air and then returning to hovering mode, which is just a touch mad?' Jonny replied.

Jonny thought momentarily and then said quietly, 'Oh, can I find the Ice Queen of Iceland in a geyser or near a geyser?'

'No,' Laughs Parps said matter-of-factly, 'you will find the Ice Queen of Iceland behind one of the biggest waterfalls in Iceland, but which one, well, that's anybody's guess.'

'It's half term soon, Jonny, so perhaps we could all go,' Sir Ranulf said as he began watering the rows of beautiful roses that gave off such a wonderfully scented aroma.

'Oh yes, what a great adventure,' Jonny replied.

'But first, it's bath time and bed for you, young man,' Lady Kathleen purred.

'Yes, and we must leave you now,' Laughs with Parps said mournfully.

'Leave? What do you mean, leave?' Jonny asked while standing up and rubbing the grass off his hands.

'Our time is up, and Big Chief Running Stool has to return to his sacred lands,' Laughs with Parps, wiping a tear from her delicate tanned skin.

'Will we see each other again?' Jonny asked sadly, almost knowing the reply already.

'In another time and place,' Big Chief Running Stool replied. 'In another time and place.' Then he and Laughs with Parps just vanished into thin air, leaving the dirty, old, weather-beaten, skin-like map on the ground. Jonny picked up the map and looked at all the strange symbols, then turned to Legend and Legion and whispered, 'Are these symbols the same as the ones written on the other map and the same writings as the ones we saw in Amaranta?'

'Perhaps they are all connected,' Legend and Legion replied in unison.

'You know, I think you are right,' Jonny replied. Jonny kissed Lady Kathleen goodnight, waved to Sir Ranulf, who was still busy with the roses and walked upstairs with Legend and Legion. He stopped off briefly to fill the old bathtub, stripped off, and jumped straight in.

'Yikes, that burns,' Jonny screamed as he leapt right out of the bath, while Legend and Legion rolled around the floor at the sight of Jonny, so-called clever Plumb, sitting in the basin pouring cold water onto his now red raw bottom.

'To hell with the bath, I'm going to bed,' Jonny scowled.

* * * * * * *

Jonny picked up his torch and checked the map from the confines of his bed as Legion and Legend happily snored in unison. The torchlight made the map seem almost transparent, something no one had noticed before, not even Laughs with Parps and her odd father, Big Chief Running Stool. Jonny smiled as he remembered the time he saw Laughs with Parps as she and her parping, self-propelled father floated around his house in absolute silence. Jonny's eyes began to close as the battery on his tiny torch ran out of power, and all fell silent, but for an owl going 'toowit toowoo' in the back garden.

* * * * * * *

Half term arrived, as it tends to do, and hordes of happy, singing, shouting and screaming children ran out of the school gates, looking forward to a few weeks' break.

Isobel grabbed Jonny's hand, and together, they walked down the leafy lanes, excitedly talking about the upcoming trip to Devon. So far, Jonny had been able to conceal the fact that he was going from Devon to Iceland, but he was still unsure if he should tell her.

'Jonny, what do I need to bring?' Isobel asked excitedly in her young voice as they made a long list of things to bring. Together, they made a song as they wound through Rutland's beautiful, leafy, birdsong-filled lanes.

'Take a toothbrush and a comb
Perhaps some loose change in case we phone
Writing paper and coloured pens
Summer days that will never end
Laughing daily while holding hands
Eating ice cream and making plans
Dodging lightning and rainy showers
Riding bareback for hours and hours
Picking bogies from our noses
Wiping them on each other's clothes
Going swimming in the sea
With only you and only me
Oh, our half-term holiday's
Such a laugh
Won't be missing
Sloppy Botty's or his very stinky parps.'

Jonny and Isobel giggled incessantly at the song they had just made up and continued to laugh and giggle at Isobel's house.

Jonny waved Isobel an excited goodbye, shouting, 'Pick you up at eight,' and then blew Isobel a kiss, which she had pretended to catch and place in her pocket.

* * * * * * *

Jonny ran the few miles home and was greeted by his two ever-so-faithful friends, Legend and Legion, who were waiting for him by the giant gates.

'Hello Legion, hello Legend,' Jonny said as he began to play-fight with them, not always a good idea at the best of times, as all too soon Jonny lay helpless, pinned down by the sheer weight of these two fully grown dogs.

'Tea's ready,' Nanny Carole shouted from the front door where Charlie was busy cleaning out the Jungle Queen, and Sir Ranulf was busy under the bonnet of Genevieve, getting them both ready for the trip ahead.

'Harry's on his way,' Jonny said, smiling. Sir Ranulf stopped working on his car and listened intently but couldn't hear a thing. Then, he could hear the steady growling engine getting louder in the distance. Soon, Sir Harry's car skidded to a halt just inches from Genevieve's bumper. He revved the engine a few times and then was silent as he turned off the ignition.

'What a racket,' Lady Kathleen said as she greeted Sir Harry and his wife Bunty.

'What a car,' Sir Harry replied, wiping off a few specks of dirt and then added, 'So, Jonny, what car would you like to drive to Devon in, my 5.7 litre all-singing all-dancing AC Shelby Cobra or the gleaming, sleek but slow Genevieve, or the ageing snail-slow parping Jungle Queen?'

'Oh, that's easy, the Jungle Queen,' Jonny replied, surprising everyone.

'Why on earth would you choose that?' Sir Harry asked.

'Well, because as we are all going together, we would all be going as fast as the slowest car, right?'

'The boy's got a point,' Sir Ranulf said proudly.

'Or perhaps I will beat you all hands down and go in the Silver Arrow Flying Spaceship. I could be there and back before you got out of first gear.'

'Want to bet?' Sir Harry replied excitedly.

'Yes, just give me a few seconds,' Jonny replied. Within a few minutes, he had run a bath, jumped in fully clothed, retrieved the Golden Globe, emptied the bath, dried himself, changed into dry clothes, and stood next to Sir Harry with the Silver Arrow Flying Spaceship glimmering in the beautiful sunny morning. In his hand, he held Legend's collar, which was made from stardust.

'What's the collar for?' Sir Harry asked.

'Oh, just to prove I got to Devon. I will leave Legend's collar around the spire of the Cathedral in Exeter.'

'Oh, I have just got to see this,' Professor Ziad's familiar voice said, walking up the drive.

'Then you can. You can come with me as further proof.'

'Oh yes, and a wibbedy wobbedy woowoo,' the Professor said excitedly.

'So, Jonny, the bet is that you will fly with the Professor three hundred plus miles to Exeter Cathedral, place the collar of stardust around the top of the spire and return here to this spot by the time Sir Harry has reached...'

'...forty miles an hour,' Sir Harry interrupted Sir Ranulf mid-sentence.

'Yep,' Jonny replied nonchalantly.

'OK, then Charlie, you walk 100 yards down the road; I will go with Sir Harry to check his speed and Lady Kathleen, when we are all ready, drop your handkerchief,' Sir Ranulf said, rubbing his hands.

'Walk in the park, old boy,' Sir Harry whispered to Sir Ranulf as they climbed into the Shelby Cobra.

'Oh, I don't know, that machine can move,' Sir Ranulf replied ruefully, pointing at the glimmering faster-than-light spaceship.

'Come on, old boy, how on earth could I lose? All I have to do is drive from zero to forty in first gear, six seconds max,' Sir Harry said with a little bit of doubt in his voice.

'OK, what's the bet?' Professor Ziad asked.

'Sportsman's bet,' Jonny replied as he and the Professor climbed on board the fastest machine ever built in the entire universe.

Sir Harry started up the engine, and it roared into life with a loud noise as Charlie briskly walked his way to approximately one hundred yards down the lane and waited.

The Silver Arrow Flying Spaceship hovered just feet above the ground in silence.

'PAL, please take us to the Cathedral of Saint Peter's, Exeter and back here within five seconds,' Jonny asked as he stood in front of this futuristic travelling machine.

'Why such a long time?' PAL replied.

'What?' Professor Ziad asked in stunned amazement and then repeated, 'What, you mean you can do it faster?'

'Oh yes, but you seem to have forgotten, Professor; I can get there and get back before I have gone,' Jonny said, smiling, 'but I think it's only fair we give them a fighting chance.'

'No, let's not,' Professor Ziad said, smiling.

'OK,' Jonny replied, smirking, 'then watch this.'

Sir Harry and Sir Ranulf sat in the shiny, all-singing, all-dancing AC Shelby Cobra, revving the massive 5.7-litre engine to the maximum. Lady Kathleen dropped the handkerchief, but before it hit the ground, the Silver Arrow Flying Spaceship vanished only to reappear before the handkerchief hit the ground and even before Sir Harry put the car in gear.

Jonny leapt out of the Silver Spaceship alongside Professor Ziad, who was sheet white and in absolute hysterics and, without a specific dog collar made from stardust, grabbed the pink handkerchief that Lady Kathleen had dropped before it even hit the ground.

'No, no, no, no, that just can't be, no it can't be, no, seriously that just cannot be,' a very, very bemused and quite visibly upset Sir Harry whined as he slowly got out of the now silent AC Shelby all-singing all-dancing Cobra.

'Tell me it's not true,' Sir Harry asked, more like pleading with Professor Ziad.

'It's true, it's all true; I wouldn't have believed it if I hadn't seen it with my own eyes, nor the few people who saw us plus,' the Professor stopped mid-sentence then, reaching into his bag, he produced ten ice creams and handed them out with 'Made from fresh Devon Cream' written on the wrappers. He continued, 'The ice cream seller and a handful of bemused onlookers.'

'What! I mean, what happened?' Sir Harry asked while removing the wrapper of his delicious ice cream.

'Well, as soon as Lady Kathleen dropped the handkerchief, I began to float. PAL had opened the viewing screen, and all I saw was a flash of brilliant, ultra-brilliant light. The next thing I knew, we were above Saint Peter's Cathedral. Jonny leant out of the spaceship and, with one hand, wrapped Legend's collar made from stardust, did the buckle up, waved to the astonished onlookers, and then gently floated down in full view of everyone. At the same time, Jonny very casually and politely ordered ten ice creams, but he forgot to pay. The next thing I knew, we were here, and the handkerchief hadn't even reached the floor. To do that, we must have been travelling faster than the speed of light, which means I should be dead because no human could withstand the G-forces.'

'I hadn't even put the car into first gear, which doesn't even take a second,' Sir Harry said with quiet resignation in his voice and then added ruefully, 'I mean, we knew it was fast, but that's beyond very fast, that's faster than very fast.'

'Ok, let's get ready to go,' Sir Ranulf said as he started to bring suitcase after suitcase from the hall, and Charlie busied himself, putting camping equipment onto the large roof rack and food into the back of the Jungle Queen.

'Sorry, Nanny Noo, but you won't be able to drive,' Charlie said as he saw her sitting in the driving seat.

Jonny got his battered old suitcase, compass, old maps, and bone ring and jumped into the front seat of the Jungle Queen and Legend and Legion sat in the back.

Professor Ziad and Lady Kathleen got into the gleaming Genevieve, and Sir Harry and Bunty climbed into his AC Cobra as Nanny Noo and her husband stood by the front door.

'Are you sure you don't want to come with us?' Lady Kathleen asked.

'No, we are happy just to look after the house while you are gone,' Nanny Noo replied as she and her husband Stan waved goodbye.

The AC Cobra was the first to roar out of the gates, followed by the sedate and quiet Genevieve, and the old jalopy Jungle Queen brought up the rear.

* * * * * * *

Soon, the three vehicles arrived outside Isobel's house, and with a toot on the Jungle Queen's horn, Isobel ran out of her house, clutching her suitcase. She quickly jumped into the front seat next to Jonny, and all three cars drove off, honking their horns and waving to Isobel's parents.

'How old is this, Professor?' Jonny asked wide-eyed with excitement as everyone stood in silent awe of the monolith called Stonehenge.

'Unsure, old boy, and also unsure why it was built and who built it and, for that matter, when they, whoever they were, built it. They say it's a place to bring your sick, but they also say it's a place to bury your dead, and then others say it's an astrological map, as the sun rises and sets between two large stones on the solstice.'

'What's a solstice?' Isobel asked.

Jonny thought momentarily and then said, 'Oh, I know, it's when there's the shortest day of the year, December, and the longest day, summer. The word solstice comes from two Latin words: sol meaning sun and sistere meaning stand.'

'Oh, you're so clever,' Isobel gushed.

'Hold on, a minute ago, you didn't know anything, and now you know everything,' Professor Ziad said cheerily.

'Well, I forgot, but then I remembered not to forget, and so I remembered,' Jonny said, and then started to ramble on and on and on about where the stones originated from, how old they were, who brought them here, and then he said, 'actually it could be a giant clock, but one that can only be seen from space.'

'Why would people over five thousand years ago want to build a clock that nobody could see or tell the time, and that could only be seen from space?'

'For the space people, silly,' Jonny replied, giggling.

'Yes, how stupid of me,' Professor Ziad replied while slapping himself on the forehead.

'But it's not the kind of clock that tells the time as in hours, minutes and seconds. It's not like a clock; it's a time machine,' Jonny said matter-of-factly.

'So, explain how it's not a clock, but it is a clock, Jonny,' the Professor said, stroking the large fifty-ton Sarson stone, which suddenly began to vibrate, making the Professor almost jump out of his shoes with fright.

'What the bally hell was that?' Sir Ranulf and Sir Harry both said it precisely at the same time.

'It knows we're here,' Jonny replied almost in a whisper.

'How does a stone circle know anything?' Isobel whispered back. Suddenly, the Professor just disappeared into thin air.

'Don't touch the stones,' Jonny shouted out loud. Still, it was too late, as first Sir Harry, then Sir Ranulf, Charlie, and Bunty just vanished into thin air, leaving just Jonny, Isobel, and Lady Kathleen, who was still sitting in the Rolls Royce painting her immaculate nails, oblivious to the fact that her husband, his best friend, the Professor, and Charlie had disappeared. Isobel started crying and whimpering, 'I want to go home, Jonny; I want my mum.'

'Ok, darling, ready,' Lady Kathleen said as she walked over to where Jonny stood with a crying Isobel.

'What on earth's the matter, Isobel? Why are you crying? Jonny, why is Isobel crying? Where's my husband? Jonny, what's happening?' Lady Kathleen asked, getting visibly upset.

'They've gone, they've all disappeared,' Isobel sobbed.

'Who's gone? What's all disappeared?' Lady Kathleen asked, looking Isobel up and down.

'Everybody,' Isobel replied almost in a whisper, slowly repeating, 'everyone.'

* * * * * * *

Meanwhile, Nanny Carole was humming along to one of her favourite Beatles songs when she heard an almighty commotion from upstairs. She quickly turned the radio's volume dial down to ensure she wasn't dreaming. She could have sworn she heard voices, so she grabbed a frying pan, quietly opened the kitchen door and tiptoed up the vast staircase, one step at a time. A heated conversation came from Jonny's bathroom, and the voices sounded very familiar.

'Hello,' she shouted as she walked up the stairs. Still, she could hear voices but no reply.

Soon, she was standing outside the bathroom. With one hand, she raised the frying pan above her head and gently tapped on the bathroom door with the other.

'Hello, I know you're in there. Come out, or I'll phone the police,' Nanny Carole shouted.

'Unlock the door,' came the reply, and the voice was instantly recognisable. It was the voice of Sir Ranulf.

'Oh my God, thank heavens it's you,' Nanny Carole said as she rushed to unlock the bathroom door, but strangely, it wasn't locked.

'The doors open,' she shouted through the door, still holding on tight to the enormous frying pan, ready to hit the first thing that emerged from within the bathroom.

The door handle rattled, and suddenly, the door flew open. Sir Ranulf, Sir Harry, Professor Ziad, Lady Bunty, and Charlie stood in the bath.

'What the!!!' Nanny Carole yelled out as she slowly walked into the bathroom. The bath was full of water; Professor Ziad, Charlie, and a fuming Lady Bunty were still standing there. All five were soaked to the skin and shivering.

'What the!!!!' Nanny Carole repeated, adding, 'But you only left here three hours ago; why did you come back? Why didn't you come back through the front door? Why are you all wet? Where is Lady Kathleen, Isobel, Jonny and the boys?'

'We, we don't know,' Sir Ranulf replied, still cold. 'One minute we were at Stonehenge, and the next,' Sir Ranulf paused for a second, looked at the other four, and then said, 'Here.'

'Quickly get out, I'll get some towels and some dry clothes,' Nanny Carole said, holding onto the frying pan. She quickly returned with warm towels and some clothes.

'I'll make a nice cup of tea,' Nanny Carole said, quickly running downstairs to the kitchen.

* * * * * * *

The four men sat around the kitchen table, sipping hot tea and eating marmalade on toast, when the discussions began in earnest.

'Okay, I think we should all say what happened,' Sir Ranulf said, adding, 'Okay, Professor, you disappeared first, you start.'

'Ok, well, all I remember was the large stone vibrating, and then I found myself in the bath.'

'Anything else?' Sir Ranulf asked quizzically.

'Well, come to think of it, I did,' the Professor said, staring into his hot tea, the heat misting up his glasses, 'I saw a giant waterfall.'

'Me too,' Sir Harry piped in.

'And me,' Charlie added.

'Yes, and me,' Lady Bunty seethed.

'Yes, that's what I remember,' Sir Ranulf said, almost whispering, then adding, 'but why did we all see a giant waterfall? Does it have some hidden meaning?'

The room went silent as they all pondered what had happened and the significance of seeing a giant waterfall.

'Well, what about your wife, Jonny, Isobel, and the boys?' Sir Harry asked, breaking the silence.

'Well, if I know Jonny, he should bring them back here, but I don't know how as my wife can't drive, and Jonny's just a bit too young. Mind you, the way things are at the moment, perhaps Legend or Legion will drive.'

'He can fly,' Charlie butted in.

'Yes, but why would he bring them back here? Perhaps they got lost as well. I mean, what if they had touched another stone and ended up somewhere else?' the Professor said, adding, 'we can't really phone the police telling them that they are all missing as they will be bound to ask too many stupid questions. They do that, and they're very good at that.' They all laughed out loud, but this wasn't a laughing matter; it was deadly serious.

'Why don't we try and reverse the journey?' Charlie said, beginning to pace up and down, visibly stressed.

'What? We all jump back in the bath and hope we end up at Stonehenge. Imagine if we ended up somewhere else?' Sir Harry argued back.

'Well, we can sit here doing diddly if you like, but I think we should at least try,' Sir Ranulf replied.

'Yes, good point, old boy. Hands up who's in favour of Charlie's idea,' Sir Ranulf said, raising his hand. Charlie raised him, as did Sir Harry and his wife, but the Professor kept his hands firmly grasping his tea.

'What's bothering you, old boy?' Sir Harry asked.

'Look at ourselves,' Professor Ziad replied.

'What, what the bally hell are you talking about?' Sir Harry retorted. 'We have aged,' Professor Ziad said sullenly.

Charlie looked at Sir Harry, Sir Harry looked at Sir Ranulf, and Sir Ranulf looked at Lady Bunty as they stood up to look into the hall mirror.

'Oh my God,' Sir Ranulf whispered as he checked his reflection. Where there was dark brown hair, there were no streaks of grey, and before, he only had a few lines on his battle-scarred face; he now had many. Soon, he was joined by four faces all staring at themselves in the mirror.

All five of them suddenly ran up the two flights of stairs, fighting to see who would get in the bath first. As Charlie was still the youngest, he arrived first and leapt headlong into the tub without even looking, followed immediately by the other four.

'What in God's name are you doing?' Lady Kathleen asked as the four men and Lady Bunty lay atop each other in an empty bathtub.

'Quickly fill the bath up,' Sir Ranulf ordered. Without hesitation, he turned the huge tap on the creaky old water boiler, thoroughly soaking everyone and ignoring his wife's pleas.

Sir Harry turned around and looked up, quickly followed by Sir Ranulf, Professor Ziad, and Charlie, who could hardly breathe.

'What are, what the, how, good grief, where did you spring from?' Sir Ranulf spluttered while trying desperately to turn the vast tap off and, failing miserably, pouring even more hot water into the quick-filling bath as poor old Charlie began almost to drown.

They all climbed out of the bath one by one with extreme embarrassment written across all their faces.

'What in the name of God are you four stupid, pig-eyed, knuckle-dragging, baboon-faced moronic chimpanzees doing?' Lady Kathleen barked, desperately trying not to laugh at the view before her, then adding, 'And Bunty, I thought you would know better.'

'Hello dear,' Sir Ranulf said sheepishly.

'Don't you say hello, dear me; where the hell have you been?' Lady Kathleen screamed back.

'Err, well, erm, well, you're not going to believe this, but erm.'

'We journeyed through a time portal,' Professor Ziad said, interrupting Sir Ranulf's stuttering.

'Did you? Did you really, you all travelled through a time porter?' Lady Kathleen replied, getting visibly angrier and angrier but finding it increasingly difficult not to laugh at the sight in front of her.

'Time portal, time portal, not an, erm, time porter,' Professor Ziad replied.

'Where's Jonny, Isobel, and the boys?' Sir Ranulf asked.

'Oh, well done for remembering our son,' Lady Kathleen shouted, but she couldn't be angry anymore. She, Lady Bunty, and everyone else just began to laugh, and they all laughed out loud for ages.

'So where is Jonny, Isobel, and the boys then?' Sir Ranulf asked while drying himself down again.

'If you hadn't been so immersed in checking your age lines and grey hair, you might have noticed him land, drive—yes, drive all the cars out, drop Isobel off home, and now he's gone back to Devon as he said he had things to do.'

'What things, and he can't be alone,' Sir Ranulf replied, sighing.

'Well, he won't get lost, fall into a time portal, turn grey and wrinkly, or end up in a bath with all his adult friends, will he? And he isn't alone as he has Legend and Legion with him,' Lady Kathleen replied vehemently.

* * * * * * *

The Silver Flying Arrow Spaceship hovered silently and invisibly just above the spire of Saint Peter's Cathedral. Silently, the door opened, and in an instant, Jonny reached out, undid the clasp on Legend's collar, and quickly stuffed it into his pocket.

'Ok, best we pay the ice cream vendor,' Jonny said, giggling as he pulled out a fresh, brand-new one-pound note that Lady Kathleen had given him, along with four more. The Silver Spaceship silently hovered a few feet from the ground as if waiting its turn to purchase more delicious ice creams. When the ice cream vendor had dealt with the last customer, the Silver Flying Arrow suddenly appeared, making the ice cream vendor push the ice cream he was about to eat right into his eye. Jonny, polite as ever, did not laugh at the ice cream vendor who stood open-mouthed as ice cream dripped from his face but instead reached out and handed the brand-new one-pound note to the astonished ice cream vendor, saying, 'Keep the change,' and in a second, was gone. The ice cream vendor quickly opened the door to his van and looked skywards, spinning around as he did, searching the heavens in vain for the boy in the Spaceship, but sadly, it and the boy were gone.

* * * * * * *

'Ok, a time portal and not a time porter, Lady Kathleen, is like a black hole or even a wormhole,' Professor Ziad said as he paced up and down in front of the enormous fireplace, puffing away on his pipe, stopping every so often to prod the hot tobacco, and then continued.

'Is a gateway, a door if you like, to another world, dimension, time, or place and it appears you have one here.'

'Yes, well, that might be, but thirty feet in the air, in an old bathtub, why there?' Sir Ranulf replied.

'Well, I don't think it's the bathtub, but it is placed strategically as a doorway, and Jonny found it.'

'Do you think Jonny knew?' Lady Kathleen asked.

'No, but he certainly found it,' Sir Ranulf said with pride in his voice. 'So can we go back to, you know, Stonehenge?' Sir Harry asked.

'What, to regain your looks,' Lady Kathleen said, laughing.

'Well, yes, actually, we have all aged ten years in less than one second. I want those ten years back,' Sir Harry said quite angrily.

'Me too, old boy,' Sir Ranulf added. Suddenly, the phone leapt to life.

'Rutland 6750,' Lady Kathleen said in her ever so posh accent.

The telephone made some strange noises, and then there was a distant voice,
'Hello, Mother.'
'Jonny, Jonny, oh Jonny, I am so happy you're safe. Oh, Jonny, how are you, Jonny? Have you eaten Jonny? Where exactly are you, Jonny?'
'Is it Jonny?' Sir Harry said, chortling.
'Ask him how he is doing,' Sir Ranulf shouted out.
'He says he's in Devon and is about to go and find a cave or something,' Lady Kathleen whispered as she placed her beautifully manicured hand across the mouthpiece.
'I have no more pennies left; I will ring you when possible. Oh, and by the way, I paid the ice cream vendor.' The phone went dead.
'Says he's fine, visiting some caves or something,' Lady Kathleen replied as she slowly placed the handset back onto the phone and whispered, 'I miss him.'

* * * * * * *

Jonny laid the dirty, old, weather-beaten map out on the floor of the Silver Arrow and gently took out the bone ring from his pocket, resting it on the map. Immediately, one solitary word that was once hidden appeared.
DUMNONII
'What does that mean, PAL?' Jonny asked, waving the old map in the air.
'It's the old name for Devon, and here's an interesting link: Alfred the Great was a Viking,' PAL replied.
'So, there's a link between Devon and Iceland?' Jonny asked.

'Yes, it would appear so,' PAL replied.

'Well, I have to find a hidden entrance at the bottom of a place called Lydford Gorge, and somewhere there is a white lady and near that, a cave, agh, a cave full of bats.'

'Why aggghh, Jonny?' PAL asked.

'I hate the dark, and I hate bats, so being in a place that's not only dark but also has bats isn't my idea of a holiday,' Jonny said, pointing at the map and its strange writings.

'Holiday! This isn't supposed to be a holiday, Jonny; this is an adventure,' PAL replied.

'Okay, well, can you drop me off near the gorge, PAL, and we will go and find the hidden cave. Are you ready, boys?'

'Did you say bats?' Legend and Legion replied, pacing up and down, then adding, 'We don't like bats that much, don't mind the dark, but bats.'

'How can you be scared of bats?' Jonny asked, amazed at the fear in both Legend and Legion's voices and then added, 'Listen, you pair of girls' blouses, you are the size of a small Dumnonii village, you are as powerful as the oceans, you are as fearsome as the night, yet you are frightened of a little bat.'

'Well, you're scared as well,' Legend said as if to justify his fears.

'Yes, I am, I admit it, but it won't stop me going for this massive adventure. We have to find a hidden song written in Icelandic. We then have to go to Iceland and find the Ice Queen, who is beautiful beyond belief and likes Rottweilers, but only brave Rottweilers and not a pair sissy Mary Rottweilers who are a pair of pink pansies scared of a little bat or two.'

'...Ahem,' PAL said, stopping Jonny in mid-rant, 'they're not so little Jonny.'
'What? What do you mean, they're not so little,' Legend and Legion replied, sitting nervously and looking at each other.
'Giant bats?' Jonny asked nervously.
'Yes, Jonny, ever so giant bats,' PAL replied matter-of-factly.
'Perhaps they're man-eating bats,' Legend said, trying to scare Jonny.
'Don't you mean boy-in-shorts eating bats,' Legion replied, sniggering.
'Oh, crumbs,' Jonny whispered to himself.
In a flash, Jonny, Legion and Legend had jumped a few feet to the ground as PAL took the Silver Spaceship skywards at incredible speed. The sun beat down on Jonny's head, and he stopped for a second to feel its warmth. He held the old map and the old bone ring in his pocket. It all seemed eerily quiet, but it was late afternoon, and most sightseers had gone home or were too busy eating fresh cream teas. Slowly, Jonny went down towards the gorge and looked down at the edge. It seemed to go down forever, and right at the bottom of the near-vertical drop, a gentle, turquoise-blue river flowed. Soon, they were knee-deep in the beautiful stream, playing and splashing, the boy-eating giant bats a distant memory. As they walked downstream, the river seemed to pick up some pace, and soon, it was just too fierce to keep wading. They all leapt out and continued walking along a winding, narrow path as the noise of distant rushing water got louder and louder. Soon, they all stood and looked up at the magnificent waterfall cascading down

shining, slippery rocks. Jonny checked his map and then took out the bone ring from his pocket and placed it next to the drawing of a waterfall, and as if by magic, the words "White Lady" suddenly appeared.

'Wow, the White Lady wasn't a lady after all; this is the white lady,' Jonny said, pointing skywards at the magnificent cascades of water crashing down a few feet before them. Jonny edged closer and immediately slipped over; the bone ring flew through the air, and as Jonny lay helpless, it silently plopped into the vast pond at the foot of the White Lady waterfall.

'Oh bother, bother, bother,' Jonny said, removing his shirt and edged towards the ice-cold water.

'Are you mad?' Legend said as he jumped headlong into the freezing waters, quickly followed by Legion. Within minutes, two soaking wet and breathless dogs emerged from the water, and in Legion's mouth was the bone ring.

'Phew, that was close,' Jonny said, taking the bone ring gently out of Legion's enormous mouth. Jonny checked the bone ring over and over again and said,

'This isn't the bone ring I dropped; this is a completely different bone ring.'

Then suddenly, the sky darkened, and the White Lady waterfall began to flow with crimson blood.

'Oh my god, Legend, what have you done?' Jonny asked while putting his shirt back on.

'Saved your life,' both Legion and Legend replied.

'What? How did jumping in there save my life?' Jonny asked, pointing at the crimson-red blood-filled pool.

'Well, if you had jumped in, you would now be dead.'

'Very dead,' Legion added.

'Yes, thank you, Legion,' Legend replied, nudging Jonny away from the crimson-red blood-filled pool.

'I, I, I don't understand,' Jonny said, still walking backwards from the water.

'Jonny, sit down and listen. The bone ring still held huge amounts of evil, which was removed by falling into the White Lady pool. However, if you had jumped in to find the ring, the evil within would have got hold of you again, the same evil that the Gnud Repeek had over you. If you look at the ring again, you will see its evil markings have been removed. Okay, Jonny, now watch this.'

Legend placed the cleansed bone ring onto the old map, and words that were hidden before emerged immediately.

'DANGER DO NOT ENTER THE DEATH POOL'

'The evil lodged within the ring tried to fool you, and it almost did,' Legion said, then added, 'and we must not enter the cave of a million bats.'

'Phew, is that because there is more evil in there?' Jonny asked.

'No, it's because it has a million giant bats in it,' Legion and Legend both replied, laughing.

'So how do I find the hidden ma...' but before Jonny could finish saying the word map, the water in the death pool began to change colour back to turquoise blue and completely vanished, leaving just an old stone staircase as the White Lady waterfall stopped running. Jonny looked at Legend and Legion and shrugged his shoulders.

'Yes, it's safe,' both Legend and Legion said in unison.

Jonny looked into the dark cavernous hole as the once-filled-to-the-brim crimson blood pool emptied. 'But we must hurry. We only have seconds to find the map. Quickly follow me,' Legion said, his every word echoing as he ran down the slippery, old, never-before-seen stone stairs, soon followed by Legend and then a very tentative Jonny.

'Did you bring the map and bone ring?' Legend shouted out, his deep voice echoing around the cavernous caves.

'Yes, yes,' Jonny replied.

'Ok, then come this way,' Legend shouted while running towards an eerie green light at the end of the cave.

'Quickly, get the ring,' Legend shouted to Jonny. Jonny went to hand the ring to Legend.

'No, don't give it to me; place it on the map.' Jonny quickly laid the old weather-beaten map on the damp cave floor and gently placed the bone ring dead centre. Suddenly, the ground began to shake louder and louder. The cave started to shudder, and rocks began to fall when suddenly the word 'LATRABJARG' appeared in shining letters on the map and the wall in front of him, the words to the song called "The Queen of Amaranta," which he had to learn and then sing to the Ice Queen of Amaranta when he eventually found her if he ever finds her, but time was running out.

'hringir í þig úr fjarlægu landi
Í hönd hennar hún heldur alheiminn
Og í hjarta hennar lykillinn að dyrum
Hún er ljós á dökkum bláum sjó
A græðandi sál sem sýnir sársauka þinn

Leyfa henni að taka þig á ferð
Gegnum þoku sem Amaranta dag
Queen Amaranta er að kalla þig
Frá langt og fjarlægu landi
Barn, fylgdu mér til a veröld af undrum
Sem þú hefur aldrei séð áður Sjáið
Queendom af Amaranta
Þar eilífðinni baðaður ljósi
Strjúka blóm sem aldrei dofnar
Samúð handan augum þínum
Svo fljúga með Queen Amaranta
Gegnum höf grænblár blár
Svífa utan anda sækni
Baða í sunsets af Amaranta
Búið bara fyrir þig.'

'How on earth am I going to remember all that?'
Jonny whispered to himself, fearful of falling under
a mass of rocks and water.
'Quickly, we must go,' Legend shouted, his voice
still echoing as all three ran like crazy towards the
old, slippery stone staircase. The cave walls
began to crumble, and the White Lady waterfall
again began to cascade with a million gallons of
ice-cold water. Jonny, Legend, and Legion
emerged just in time to see the underwater cave
system filled with water.
'Crumbs and crikey, that was close,' Jonny said
and then, quick as you could say
"antidisestablishmentarianism," all three ran back
up the gorge to the awaiting Silver Flying Arrow.
'To Latrabjarg, to Latrabjarg,' Jonny said
breathlessly. The Silver Flying Arrow silently
turned on its axis.

'Hold on,' Jonny shouted, immediately disappearing from the open door and returning with three large cream teas in seconds.

'Ok, PAL, to LATRABJARG.'

The Silver Flying Arrow pointed skywards and was gone in a flash of brilliant light and phenomenal power.

CHAPTER THREE:
THE CLIFFS AT THE END OF THE EARTH...

Silently, the Silver Flying Arrow Spaceship hovered above the Cliffs at the end of the Earth, also known as the Cliffs of Latrabjarg.

Jonny, Legend, and Legion stood silently and gazed at the incredible sight before them. The sheer cliff face was almost one mile high and seemed to stretch to infinity. The mighty, freezing winds that swept across the North Atlantic Ocean far below them crashed into the rock with incredible force, leaving spumes of seawater over one hundred metres high.

Jonny laid the old map on the floor and studied it intently as Legion and Legend stared at the wildlife perching high on the cliffs.

'So, where are we?' Jonny asked PAL while pointing at the map.

'Northwest Iceland,' PAL replied.

'Oh, great help,' Jonny replied sarcastically, then added, 'I mean, where are we on this map, as Latrabjarg isn't on it?'

'Well, it wouldn't be, would it, as that map is probably thousands upon thousands of years old,' Legend piped in.

'He's got a point,' Legion added.

'I know, what if I warm it up? That worked with the other map and the disc,' Jonny said, then added, 'PAL, can you heat this small section of the floor?'

Suddenly, the map took on an entirely new look.

'What the...!!!!?' Legend stuttered.

'Yes, what the, indeed,' Legion replied.

Jonny stood up to get a better view of the strange markings.

'Okay, well, I can't understand any of it, plus I have to decipher that song from Icelandic into English. Any help, PAL, would be greatly appreciated,' Jonny asked, hopefully.

'The map's three dimensional,' PAL said matter of factly.

'Oh, great help, so what exactly does that mean?' Jonny replied, getting slightly miffed.

'You must find and wear some three-dimensional glasses,' Legend added.

'Do you have a pair, Legend, Legion?' Jonny asked, slowly losing the will to live.

'Well, let me just check my handbag,' Legend replied.

'Oh yes, and let me check mine as well,' Legion said, then added sarcastically.

'Dang, we both forgot to bring our three-dimensional glasses; wow, what a silly mistake. I brought sun lotion, nail varnish, curlers and clean underwear, but I forgot my three-dimensional glasses in my rush. What about you, Legend?'

'Yep, me too, but I have my toothbrush and a comb, false teeth, talcum powder for nappy rash, an old sock and a biscuit,' Legend said, smirking.

'Biscuit! You have a biscuit?' Legion asked and then jumped over Legend, pretending to fight for the imaginary biscuit in Legend's giant paws.

'Ok, ok, so you don't have any three-dimensional glasses then?' Jonny asked, almost resigned to give up this adventure before it started.

'Make a pair,' PAL said.

'Yes, okay. I will find some glass, cut it into shape, and then invent something I have never seen before,' Jonny replied while slapping his forehead with his open hand. Then he realised he had seen a pair before, as Professor Ziad had made one. 'Why did you go to those nine planets, Jonny?' Legend and Legion asked in unison.

'To learn,' but before Jonny could finish his words, a sudden if not a rare, flash of intelligence hit him. 'Do we have any blue or red plastic, PAL?' Jonny asked.

'We do now,' PAL replied, and out of thin air, two small sheets of red and blue plastic landed silently onto the transparent floor.

Jonny ignored Legend and Legion, who were acting up something rotten, probably from boredom.

Jonny tore the plastic into small squares and placed the blue plastic over his right eye and the red piece over his left. Suddenly, the map transformed from an odd, old, greying, torn and decrepit waste of time to the most jaw-dropping, lung-bursting, hair-raising, head-banging, knee-knocking, parp-making work of stunning beauty he had ever seen. Sadly, for Jonny, it was written entirely in Icelandic.

'Great,' Jonny said as the two bits of plastic dropped from his eyes and gently floated in the air.

'Great, what? Balls of fire?' Legend asked.

'Great googlie wooglies?' Legion added.

'Great Missenden?' Legend said, nearly wetting himself, giggling.

'Great lakes?' Legion added, unable to contain himself anymore, as Jonny's massive servants were reduced to infantile giggling. Jonny looked on with pity in his eyes.

'Walkies?' Jonny shouted, and Legend and Legion immediately came to heel.

'PAL, land on top of the cliffs so the boys can remove some of the travel silliness they appear to have found,' Jonny ordered.

In a split second, the Silver Arrow Spaceship had landed gracefully. Legend and Legion jumped out and ran up and down the massive cliffs in sheer joy and excitement. Jonny looked again at the map, but this time, in perfect peace.

'Seems to be a starting point, here,' Jonny said, pointing to the base of the Cliffs at the end of the Earth, 'and then it seems to go up. Oh, you don't think it means I have to climb the mile-high cliffs, do you?' Jonny said with slight trepidation in his voice.

'Yes, it would appear so,' PAL replied.

'Great,' Jonny said, sighing.

'What's that snake-looking thing?' PAL asked.

'I don't know, but it's enormous, and the word written next to it says LAGRFLJOTSORMURNN, pronounced LAG-R-FLIOT-SOR-MURNN,' Jonny replied.

'Enormous isn't the word I would use, Jonny, because if this map is to scale, then that snake thing is five miles long.'

'F-f-f-five miles long?' Jonny said stuttering.

'The boys are back,' PAL said as he opened the door, and the two out-of-breath dogs ran back in.

'Wow, that was exhilarating,' Legend said, panting out loud.

'Not as exhilarating as that,' Jonny said, pointing to the snake.

'What's that?' Legend asked in mild surprise.

'Oh, just a snake that's five miles long,' Jonny replied.

'Well, if that snake is five miles long, then what on earth is that?' Legion asked, pointing at a massive, colossal being.

'It's a Troll,' PAL replied all matter of factly.

'What's a Troll?' Legend asked.

'That is,' Jonny replied and then added. 'It seems I have to climb the Cliffs at the end of the Earth, then climb a ten-mile-high volcano, swim in the boiling rivers of REKJADALUR...'

'Jonny, there are many volcanos in Iceland, and all of them are huge,' PAL butted in and then reeled off a list of all their names. 'KOLBEINSEY RIDGE, TJORNES FRACTURE ZONE, THEISTAREYKJARBUNGA, KRAFLA, FREMRINAMUR, ASKJA, LYSUHOLL, LJOSUFJOLL, SNAEFELLSJOKULL, HOFSJOKULL VOLCANO...'

'Ok, I think we get the picture, PAL. There are many volcanos, but which one do I have to climb?'

'KATLA is the largest, or ORAEFAJOKULL, which is the most violent,' PAL replied.

'Great,' Jonny said, slumping down to the floor and adding, 'So what else have I got to do?'

'Translate the song?' Legend said.

'Ok, well, let's find a hiding place for the Silver Arrow, and then I can start translating the song and get some much-needed sleep,' Jonny said with resignation in his young voice.

PAL manoeuvred the faster-than-light spaceship to the base of the mile-high cliffs, where they found a large enough cave to hide. Jonny translated the song while PAL swatted about Iceland, and Legion and Legend fell fast asleep.

Jonny sat tapping his pencil against his teeth, but for his life, he couldn't remember the song's first line, let alone all of it.

'If I could only remember the first few words,' he mumbled to himself. Then Jonny tried going through the alphabet until he remembered the first letter, so Jonny began with 'A, B, C, D, E, F, G, H, M. H sounds familiar, so Jonny wrote down H.

'Oh God, this will take forever,' Jonny whined.

'How about, hringir í þig úr fjarlægu landifamiliar,' a familiar voice echoed around the Silver Arrow Spaceship.

'Cosmos, is that you?' Jonny asked quickly, turning to his left and right.

'Yes, but I can say no more, except drottningu af Iceland, the Queen of Iceland.'

'Cosmos, Cosmos, COSMOS,' Jonny shouted while searching high and low.

'He has gone,' PAL said gently.

Suddenly, Jonny saw the words written in flames right before him. Jonny could almost feel the heat and reached to touch them as his little fingers passed through the vision. Jonny quickly scribbled down the words...

'The Queen of Iceland
Calls you from a distant shore
In her hand, she holds the universe
And in her heart, the key to the door
She is the light of the dark blue oceans
A healing soul who reveals your pain
Allow her to take you on a journey
Through the mists of an Icelandic day
The Queen of Iceland is calling you
From a far and distant shore
Child, follow me to a world of wonders

That you have never seen before
Behold the Queendom of Iceland
Where eternity is bathed in light
Caress the flower that never fades
Compassion beyond your sight
So fly with the Queen of Iceland
Through the seas of turquoise blue
Soar beyond the spirits of affinity
Bathe in the sunsets of Iceland
Created just for you.'
'Don't forget to learn it word for word in English and Icelandic, as she may well ask you for both,' PAL reminded Jonny.
'Great,' Jonny replied.
'Bedtime, Jonny,' PAL said gently. Out of nowhere, the world's most comfortable, almost invisible bed, made from pure light, appeared. Jonny removed his clothes, lay on the light bed, and soon fell asleep.
'Breakfast is ready,' PAL said as two slices of warm toast covered in dripping honey floated just in front of Jonny's twitching nose, soon followed by a glass of ice-cold milk.
Jonny tucked in as Legend and Legion silently ate every morsel of dog food, which automatically arrived via a hidden chute.
'This is one clever spaceship,' Jonny said with his mouth crammed full of honey-soaked toast.
'It certainly is,' PAL replied, 'and you need to move on because today you have to start climbing, but there's one slight problem.'
'What one slight problem?' Jonny replied.
'Well, the one slight problem is, we are underwater, and you will have to swim to the surface and climb the mile-high Cliffs at the end of

the Earth. When you reach the top, you can start searching for the Queen of Iceland, not forgetting you will have to walk for days with only the food you can carry.'

'Well, that's ok; Legend and Legion can help,' Jonny replied with just a hint of uncertainty in his young voice.

'Well, if we weren't stuck in a vast cave surrounded by billions of gallons of ice-cold water and icebergs, yes, they could, but sadly, we are stuck, and before you ask, Legend and Legion, irrespective of their vast strength and size, cannot climb a vertical cliff,' PAL said matter-of-factly.

'Great, got any more bad news to wake my day?' Jonny replied while getting dressed.

'Well, come to think of it, Jonny, I have,' PAL replied as Legend and Legion tittered like silly teenagers.

'Yeah, laugh it up, titter away, you pair of crumbdumbnuts,' Jonny said as what he had to do began to hit home.

'We can join you at the top of the mile-high cliff though. Well, that's if you reach the top of the mile-high cliff. Some quite nasty, aggressive, evil monsters live on the cliff face,' Legend said, pretending to be scary.

'Not forgetting the huge seabirds,' Legion added.

'Well, more like sea vultures than seabirds, actually, Legion.'

'You're right, Legend; they are more like flying dinosaurs than birds, Angkas.'

'Sorry, what did you call me?' Jonny said, grinning.

'Angka's,' Legion replied, then added, 'and they usually fly in pairs.'

'Pair of Angka's,' Jonny replied, trying to stifle his laugh, but sadly, it was just too late, as all three of them rolled around the floor in absolute hysterics. Ten minutes passed when the order was finally restored, and Jonny prepared himself for the climb of a lifetime. PAL had to work out the tide times to manoeuvre the Silver Spaceship from deep within the cave's confines.

'Tide goes out in approximately two hours, Jonny, so you had better go now. You won't need the map, just some sturdy shoes. Do you have any sturdy shoes, Jonny?'

'Err, no, just flips flops and these,' Jonny replied, while pointing at his school plimsolls and then, after thinking for a minute, asked a fundamental question that no one had thought of asking before, which was, 'Why do I have to climb the mile-high Cliffs at the end of the Earth?'

'Because the map tells you to, silly,' Legend replied.

'Oh well, I just wondered,' Jonny replied.

'I think we should just recheck the map,' PAL said, then added, 'just in case.'

Jonny laid the map out again on the floor and then placed the blue and red plastic strips over his eyes.

'Ooops,' Jonny said, removing the plastic discs from his eyes.

'Oops, what?' Legend asked.

'Oops, it seems I have to collect certain objects, and the first one is halfway up the mile-high Cliffs at the end of the Earth.'

'Lucky you rechecked, Jonny, and be careful of the Angkas,' Legion said while smirking.

'And the hairy growlers, don't want to be caught by them,' Legend added, laughing.

'Anything else?' Jonny asked, changing into his rather worn-out plimsolls.

'Yes, Gobbler, the greedy goblin,' PAL replied, stifling his laughter.

'You're just making this up as you go along, right?' Jonny asked, getting visibly annoyed. Jonny rechecked the map to ensure the boys were telling the truth.

'Oh, it's true; there is a Gobbler, the greedy goblin, and not forgetting the five-mile-long snake, the Lagrfljotsormurnn. Oh, and its name is Rabidmutrec, and apparently, it has a lisp and a stammer. I can't wait to meet that,' Jonny said with mild surprise.

'Jonny, you need to think about setting off soon. So do you know where you're going yet?' PAL asked.

'Well, I have to climb the mile-high Cliffs at the end of the Earth and find, well, I don't know what I have to find because I can't decipher that,' Jonny replied, pointing at the map.

Legend, Legion stared at the strange markings, and then PAL said, 'Hold it up so I can see it.' Jonny held the rotten old map in the air. There were a few moments of pause as PAL studied the old weather-beaten map and said, 'They're runes, exceptional stones, and it looks like you have to collect...'

... 'Prunes,' Legend said, interrupting PAL mid-sentence, 'why would anyone in their right mind want to collect prunes?'

'How many prunes do I have to collect PAL?' Jonny asked as he was slowly losing the will to live.

'Runes, Jonny, thirteen Runes, Jonny. I don't think you will find many prunes in Iceland,' PAL replied.

'Ok, so up the cliffs, along this winding path, cross that river, swim in that river, walk over the volcanic fields, then along another winding path. Then, climb that glacier field, find that huge cave behind that huge scary-looking waterfall, meet the snake with the lisp and stammer, and then find the hidden cave. Then find the Queen of Iceland and sing her this song in either English or Icelandic or both while dodging the Angkas, the Hairy Growlers, the Greedy Gobblers, the sea monster, the Rabidmutrec, the Huldufock or the Hidden People, the Lagarfljot Worm, Trolls and be home by teatime.'

'Yep, pretty much sums it up, Jonny, but you forgot the Icelandic Yule family, thirteen children all peculiar, and parents that shouldn't have been allowed to raise a plant, let alone thirteen weird children,' PAL replied dryly, then added, 'so Legend and Legion will meet you at the top of the cliff in just over one hour.'

'Right, fifteen weirdoes, eh? I suppose you made that up, too?' Jonny said, laughing.

'Nope,' PAL replied.

'Yeah, right; well, what are their names then?' Jonny sneered.

'Ok, well, here goes. Stkkjastaur, also known as Sheep-Cote Clod, likes to harass sheep but is slightly impaired by his stiff peg legs...'

... 'Sounds like my kind of weirdo,' Legend butted in.

'Then there's Giljagaur or Gully Gawk, who likes to hide in gullies and wait for any opportunity to sneak into cowsheds.'

'Harass the cows?' Legion asked, giggling.

... 'Steal milk,' PAL added and then continued...

'Stufur or Stubby, who, as you could guess by his name, is abnormally short and loves to steal pans...'

... 'and harasses them?' Legend butted in while trying to stop giggling.

'No, eats the crusts,' PAL added, trying to be serious, but even a sedate computer found it hard not to giggle.

'Oh, I want to marry him,' Legion said, laughing out loud.

'Too late, as I've already asked him,' Legend replied, rolling around the floor, trying desperately not to wet himself.

'Well, if you thought those three were odd, wait till you hear about these guys,' PAL said, trying to regain some seriousness, but that would be very hard as Legion, Legend, and Jonny were all doubled up on the floor in hysterics.

'Ok, then there's Pvoruslelkir or Spoon Licker, who steals wooden spoons and harasses them, no I mean licks them, and is extremely thin due to malnutrition. Then there's Pottasleielkir, yes, a pot licker, who, yes, you guessed it, steals leftovers from pots. Then there's Askaslelkir, who will steal your bowl the second you put it down. Oh, and this one's my favourite: Huroaskellir, the door slammer, likes nothing more than slamming doors in the middle of the night. Then there's Skyrgamur the Skyr-Gobbler who gobbles skyr...'

... 'Seems to be a lot of gobbling going on,' Jonny shouted in near hysterics, then added, 'How many more? I don't think I can take much more of this; my God, what were their parents thinking?'

'Ok, just a few more,' PAL said, then continued, 'Bjugnakraekir, the Sausage-Swiper who hides in the attic waiting to swipe the sausages being smoked.'

'Anyone tried to swipe your sausage, Legend?' With tears rolling down his giant face, Legion asked, 'Or have you got it well hidden?'

Legend couldn't reply as he was far too busy rolling around the floor in fits of laughter.

'Ok, ok, only a few to go. There's Gluggagaegir the Window-Peeper, then Gattepefur the Doorway Sniffer.'

'No, no, enough. I can't take this anymore. Who on god's earth would want to be a doorway sniffer?' Jonny shouted out.

PAL continued. 'Ketkrokur, also known as a meat hook, uses a hook to steal meat, then there's Kertasnikir, the candle stealer, who steals candles to eat, and now, the parents. The Father of this tribe of misfits is called Leppaluol, who is just useless, and his wife Gryla, oh my God, she is as mad as an open tin of sardines and is evil as evil can be, and man, is she one plug-ugly donkey.'

In the next half hour, no one moved for insane giggling, and some of the sillier names were repeated, such as doorway sniffer and sausage swiper.

'Ok, I'm ready,' Jonny said, holding the old stinky map, the two bits of blue and red plastic, a duffle bag with a compass, dry clothes, a towel, some food and a drink.

'Hold on, Jonny, we can leave this cave. While we laughed so much, the tide has eased, which means you won't have to swim to the surface in the ice-cold waters, but you will have to be quick. As soon as I open the door, you must jump out and climb as fast as possible to find the first of the hidden runes. According to the map, they talk, so you should hear them before seeing them.'

Suddenly, there was a massive surge of power as the Silver Arrow Spaceship managed to free itself from the confines of the cave it was momentarily trapped in, and gently, it silently drifted to the surface.

'Oops,' PAL said, hoping no one would hear him.

'Ooooops, what do you mean, Ooooops?' Jonny asked.

'You know I said we were trapped inside a cave?' PAL asked.

'Yes,' Jonny, Legend and Legion all replied as one.

'Well, it wasn't a cave,' PAL said while trying to hide his embarrassment.

'Ok, if it wasn't a cave, what was it?'

'An Aspidoceleon and it's huge, no bigger than huge, and we're in its stomach,' PAL replied.

'Then get us out,' Jonny said impatiently.

'Can't,' PAL replied solemnly.

'Why?' Legend, Legion and Jonny asked in perfect unison.

'Well, we would either have to kill it or wait until it's fed and then let nature take its course.'

'Unsure I want to kill it,' Jonny replied but added, 'and the bit about nature taking its course, does that mean we have to wait until...'

... 'It's dropped the kids off, parked its breakfast, and squeezed a Malteser,' Legend said, giggling. 'Well, yes, but that could take ages,' PAL replied. 'Oh, I know, why don't we fill its stomach full of wind, and then we wait a few moments until it breaks wind, well hurricane more like,' Jonny suggested.

'Great idea, and I think it's our only choice right now,' PAL said.

PAL went to work getting the Silver Arrow Spaceship to produce enough wind so that, with a lot of luck, they could all be blown clean out of the Aspidoceleon's butt.

* * * * * * *

Meanwhile, back in the leafy lanes of Little Plopping, Isobel was walking to the local post office to collect a book she had ordered before Jonny went away.

'Hello, Isobel, there's a parcel for you here,' said the kindly Miss Dangleguts, who was quite deaf and smelled like turpentine.

'Oh, thank you, Miss Dangleguts, it's a book for my boyfriend Jonny. I'm going to give it to him when he comes home,' a very excited Isobel replied, beaming from ear to ear.

'Oh, what kind of book is it?' Miss Dangleguts asked, stroking her manky old pussy, which she called piddle puddle, while completely ignoring what Isobel had said.

'Oh, it's a book about space,' Isobel replied.

'Drains?' The slightly deaf Miss Dangleguts asked, 'Why would your horse want a book about drains?'

'No, it's a book for my boyfriend, not my horse,' Isobel replied, trying ever so hard not to laugh. 'Who on Earth would buy a book about grain for their moose?' Miss Dangleguts repeated as she shuffled to the back of the store to collect the parcel.

'No, not a moose,' Isobel replied, holding her hand over her mouth to hide her giggling.

'You have a moose, and you called her Ronnie?' Miss Dangleguts asked, getting visibly annoyed.

'Jonny,' Isobel replied in near hysterics.

'Runny?' Miss Dangleguts asked as she shuffled to the counter carrying the small parcel.

'Jonny,' Isobel replied, giggling.

'Ploppy?' Miss Dangleguts said while inspecting the parcel. 'Jonny,'

'Runny Ploppy, Butty Hopper?'

'Jonny,' Isobel repeated and then decided that now would be a great time to leave as she could hardly stand up for giggling. She held the book in her right hand and merrily skipped down the road. The sun was shining, and the birds were singing in the trees. Isobel knelt, picked some daisies from the grass verge, and then started singing a little song for the birds...

'Hello little robin
Singing in the trees
Hello little robin
Are you singing just for me?
Hello little blackbird
Chirping in the tree
Hello little robin
Are you singing just for me?
Hello little chaffinch
Tweeting in the trees

Hello, robin and blackbird
Are you singing for just me?
Hello baby thrush
Chirping in the trees
Hello, robin, blackbird and chaffinch
Are you singing for just me?'
Isobel didn't hear the runaway tractor rolling
towards her or the frantic shouts of Farmer
Piggbottom.
'LOOK OUT, LOOK OUT,' Farmer Piggbottom
shouted, waving frantically and jumping up and
down, but sadly to no avail.

* * * * * * *

'Miss Dangleguts, there's been a terrible accident.
Please phone for an ambulance,' Farmer
Piggbottom asked. It was more like shouting in
near hysteria as he ran into the Post Office. Sadly,
Miss Dangleguts misheard him and went out the
back of the post office and brought out a pack of
nappies.
'No, not nappies, you weather-beaten, ancient
crustacean, an AMBULANCE,' Farmer Piggbottom
shrieked. Miss Dangleguts pointed to the old
telephone on the counter.
Farmer Piggbottom picked up the receiver to hear
absolutely nothing. He frantically shouted down
the phone, 'Hello, hello, operator.'
'Shout as much as you like; it doesn't work, never
has,' Miss Dangleguts said, holding the
unconnected loose wire in her hand.
Farmer Piggbottom stormed out of the Post office,
seething with rage, his face red and blotchy. He
ran over to see Isobel's lifeless body still clutching

the few daisies that she had just collected. He pressed the horn of the tractor again and again. The birds had all stopped singing, and there wasn't a sound to be heard.

'Right, best I run to the nearest house,' he muttered to himself, unsure which way to go and which house had a telephone. Then he remembered there was a bell where the old fire station used to be before they built a brand new one some miles down the lane. He gently picked up Isobel's limp and lifeless body and ran hell for leather down the winding lanes until he eventually got to the old fire station. He gently put Isobel onto an old wooden table and then placed her in the recovery position. He quickly checked to see if she was breathing, but it was impossible to tell. He looked around and saw an old piece of broken glass on the ground and held it in front of her mouth; yes, the glass steamed up; she was still breathing, but only just. He then felt her pulse; it was feeble, but at least she had one. He then picked up this considerable iron bar and began to smash the enormous bell as hard and fast as he could; again and again, he hit it as it went clang clan clanging across the silent countryside. Farmer Piggbottom continued to use every inch of his immense strength to hit the bell repeatedly. Suddenly, his faithful old sheepdog Sasha appeared and instantly knew what to do, and with lightning speed, she leapt over one gate and across one field, then another. Sasha crossed the swollen river, ran past children playing on the bank side and eventually got to Little Plopping Police station, ran straight through the open doors and barked incessantly until Pc Floppy appeared with a cup of tea in his hand.

'Sasha, old girl, what on earth's the matter,' he asked, placing the cup and saucer onto the desk and bending over to stroke a very excited and panting dog. Sasha grabbed PC Floppy's shirt sleeve without warning and tugged as hard as possible. Pc Floppy wasn't the brightest of men, but he knew something was seriously wrong. Together, they ran past the children playing on the banks of the swollen river and crossed both fields to where Farmer Piggbottom was still smashing the hell out of the old fire station bell. Suddenly, out of nowhere, it seemed half the population of Little Plopping had heard the commotion, and luckily, Nurse Udders was there as well.

'Ok, ok, you can stop hitting the bell now, Harry,' his kindly wife Radish said to him.

Farmer Piggbottom, not known for his emotion, started openly crying out loud.

'I couldn't stop the tractor, I couldn't stop the tractor, I couldn't stop the tractor,' he wailed as tears rolled down his hard-as-nails face.

Soon, the ambulance arrived and screeched to a sudden halt. The ambulance men carried the stretcher to Isobel, where Nurse Udders held Isobel's delicate hand while whispering, 'It's okay, Isobel, it's okay, everything is going to be alright.' Isobel did not respond as they gently put her body into the ambulance and drove off at high speed.

'I had better go and tell her parents,' Pc Floppy said as he ran back over the two fields across the swollen river, where the children had now stopped playing.

* * * * * * *

'Rutland 6750,' Lady Kathleen purred.

'Lady Kathleen, this is Doctor Doughnut; now prepare for some bad news. There's been a terrible accident. Isobel has been run over and is now in a coma. As I speak, she is being transferred to Great Ormond Street Hospital in London.

'Oh no, what on earth happened? Is she going to be alright? Wait, let me get Sir Ranulf,' Lady Kathleen said, trying to remain calm.

'What's the matter, old sausage? Who is it?' Sir Ranulf asked, hearing the fear in his wife's trembling voice.

'It's Isobel, she, she's been run over.'

'Quickly, we must go and see her,' Sir Ranulf said, running out of the front door to the garage.

Genevieve started with a gentle purr as Sir Ranulf quickly drove out of the garage and beeped the car's horn.

'How can we contact Jonny?' Lady Kathleen asked Sir Ranulf as they swiftly drove out of the gates and sped towards London.

'I don't know, and we also don't know when he will come home. Plus, to make things worse, we can't contact him,' Sir Ranulf replied, adding, 'best I contact Eddie Rockhard.'

* * * * * * *

Genevieve pulled into the grounds of Great Ormond Street Hospital just as Isobel's parents, Lord and Lady Taylor, were getting out of their gleaming Bentley. All four were immediately ushered directly to the Flower Ward through the front entrance.

Isobel's motionless body was attached to wires, tubes and a machine that went beep, beep, beep, along with other machines. Lady Taylor, visibly shaken, began to weep uncontrollably, repeating, 'My child, my child, why God, why?'

Sir Ranulf took Lord Taylor to one side and whispered,

'Bad show, old boy, but don't give up; I know just the person to help.'

'Your son?' Lord Taylor whispered back.

'Yes, but the trouble is, he's in Iceland. I will have to get Eddie Stoneface and some of his highly trained men to go and find him.'

'That could take days, old boy,' Lord Taylor replied, almost whispering.

Lady Kathleen and Taylor sat on each side of the sleeping Isobel and gently held her hands.

'This wouldn't have happened if it wasn't for your so-called special son,' Lady Taylor hissed across the bed.

'How dare you blame our son,' Lady Kathleen hissed back.

'Well, if you're holier than thou son was here and not away wasting his time gallivanting around the world talking to trees, this would never have happened to my darling Isobel, you grotty old goat,' Lady Taylor said, raising her voice a little. At the same time, her chubby face grew redder and redder.

'Listen here, you hideous harridan, how dare you talk to me like that, you evil parping puff adder.'

'Parping? How dare you insinuate that I parp, you grossly overweight, wobble-bottomed baboon.'

'Overweight, me? How dare you say that when you're the size of an African elephant.'
'Well, at least I don't look like my face is on fire, and someone put it out with a pitchfork.'
'Well, with a face like yours, I wish I was blind.'
'Well, I don't look like a bulldog chewing an angry wasp.'
'Well, you're so hairy you look as if you have Bigfoot in a headlock.'
'Don't you just love nature despite what it did to you?'
'Rancid, raccoons, bottom burp.'
'Flatulent Hippo.'
'Ladies, ladies, can you keep the hissing down? We're trying to think here,' Sir Ranulf whispered.
'Well, we must go,' Sir Ranulf said, shaking Lord Taylor's hand. Then added, 'Don't worry, old boy, we will soon get Isobel back to normal and all ticketyboo again.'
'Thanks, old boy, thanks for dropping by, and if there's any news, ring me,' Lord Taylor replied.
'Well, goodbye, Lady Taylor. It's always lovely to meet you both,' Lady Kathleen whispered as she walked out of the hospital door, followed by Sir Ranulf.

* * * * * * *

Genevieve gently purred as they drove out of the hospital gates and towards home when Lady Kathleen asked, 'If my memory serves me right, which it normally does, didn't Professor Ziad make copies of the one hundred phials?'

'You know, my little sausage, I think you might be right, but aren't the original phials still under Jonny's bed?'
'Well, let's go and see,' Lady Kathleen replied as they drove back home through the stillness of the night.

* * * * * * *

'Is she alright?' Nanny Carole asked Lady Kathleen while serving breakfast.
'Well, she is in a coma as well as being on a life support system. Her brain is slowly dying, so we must get help as soon as possible.'
'Just rang Eddie. He's getting a four-person team prepped but couldn't get a pilot at such short notice. So, I have asked Sir Harry to accompany me. We will fly to Iceland in approximately five hours,' Sir Ranulf said as he walked into the kitchen and added...
'Darling, I have looked under Jonny's bed, and the phials are there, but there appears to be some force field protecting them. The funny thing is, when I went to touch them, I got a hell of an electric shock, so I thought it wise to leave the bally things alone. Can you quickly ring Professor Ziad and pick up Sir Harry as I go?'
Lady Kathleen walked, almost floated, into the lounge, where she dialled Professor Ziad's number.
Brrring Brrring - Brrring Brrring – Brrring Brrring.
'Hello, Professor Ziad speaking, how may I help?'
'Oh, hello, Professor, it's Lady Kathleen here. I am so sorry to bother you, but my husband and I were

just wondering if you had made DNA copies of the one hundred phials that Jonny owned.'

'Funny enough, old girl, I am doing them right now, well not. Right now, I'm trying to stop Philomena from eating any more sprouts, a hell of a job.'

'And you know how to use them? The phials, not the sprouts?' Lady Kathleen asked.

'Good grief, no idea at all,' the Professor added.

'Oh, that's not good news,' Lady Kathleen said despondently.

'Why, what's the problem?'

'The problem is... well, Isobel is in a coma. Jonny is out of the country, and we were hoping that with your help, we could bring her back to life.'

'I'm unsure that I am qualified, but I can try but knowing which one is which and how best to administer them,' Professor Ziad said almost apologetically.

'Well, one made that criminal Dodgy Dave from Dartford big, and his side kicks younger. So, what you want is the one that brings back life. Have you no idea at all, as time isn't on our side,' Lady Kathleen pleaded.

'Listen, seeing it's an emergency, I will drive to the laboratory today and see what I can do. I will ring you as soon as I get some news. Bye for now,' Professor Ziad said as he gently placed the receiver down.

* * * * * * *

The Professor left Philomena and her bowl of sprouts and terrible flatulence and hurriedly drove to his laboratory. Soon, he ran into the pristine laboratory, locking the doors and windows and closing all the blinds. He pressed the combination code to his secret safe, and out popped one hundred DNA Petri dishes, each containing a very minuscule amount of the precious serums.

'I need an injured animal,' the Professor whispered and immediately rang the local vets. Luckily, they had just brought in an injured duck about to be put to sleep.

'I'll take him,' the Professor shouted down the line, then quickly added, 'ok, I'll take her then,' and ran out of the laboratory at breakneck speed.

* * * * * * *

'She was found about thirty minutes ago. It looks like her neck might be broken, but you are more than willing to take her. She has been heavily sedated, so she is in no pain, but to be honest, I really can't see her improving. Be sure to let me know how you get on. I know you are a very clever man, Professor Ziad. You are a very clever man indeed,' the vet said gently. The Professor pushed a crisp five-pound note into the vet's hand, picked up the duck and gently carried it out to his old battered Mini.

'It's okay, it's okay,' the Professor gently reassured the frail-looking duck, then added, with genuine pride in his voice, 'I shall call you Dora after my dear Mother. ' Then he stroked the sleeping duck and quickly drove back to the laboratory.

* * * * * * *

'Did you manage to speak with the Professor?' Sir Ranulf asked as he walked into the lounge with Sir Harry.

'Yes darling, but he's as mad as a tin of open sardines, so don't expect any miracles, but he did say he would try his best,' Lady Kathleen replied while stroking Rabbcat.

'Well, Eddie and his men will be here soon, and then we leave in about four hours, so let's hope the Professor comes up with something soon.'

* * * * * * *

The Professor hid Dora under his raincoat but didn't realise that Dora had woken and had stuck her head out of the front of his raincoat, which gave the security guard a bit of a shock.

The Professor rushed up the stairs to his laboratory and gently placed the tired, half-asleep Dora onto a warm blanket. He then began concocting a cure for Dora, hoping it would also cure Isobel. Over the next half hour, he placed one phial after another under Dora's beak, but nothing seemed to be working. That was until the second to last one, which the Professor again held under Dora's beak. Dora shook her head, stood up, and then, unbelievably, started walking around.

'Oh my God, wibble wobble wabble, by Jove, I think I've done it,' the Professor shouted out loud while leaping up and down.

'Oh my god, wibble wobble wabble, by Jove, I think he's done it,' Dora replied.

'What, what wha, what did you say, old girl,' the Professor said, stuttering in absolute disbelief as he kneeled beside Dora. Then, to his utter disbelief, Dora started to sing in perfect Hebrew while dancing around the pristine laboratory.

'Hávanagíla, hávanagíla
Hávanagíla, venismechá
Hávanagíla, hávanagíla
Hávanagíla, venismechá
Hávaneránena, hávaneránena
Hávaneránena, venismechá
Hávaneránena, hávaneránena
Háva neránena, venismechá.'

Unbeknownst to the Professor, the security guard watched from the door, which he had forgotten to lock in his haste.

'Everything alright?' the security guard asked with a slight grin.

'Ye yes, yes of course,' the Professor replied, desperately trying to think of a good excuse for the Hebrew singing duck.

'Did you like my singing?' the Professor asked, hoping the security guard hadn't heard it was Dora the singing duck singing.

'Preferred the ducks,' the security guard replied dryly.

'Listen, old boy, not a word, top secret, need to know, mum's the word.'

'As it's you, Professor, my lips are sealed, but I must ask Hebrew!

Why in Hebrew?

'Because that's the language it was written in, lugnuts,' Dora, the Hebrew-singing duck, replied.

Professor Ziad threw some cold water over the now passed-out security guard, who came around with a jolt.

'It's ok, old boy. It must have been the heat. You appear to have passed out, but you'll be fine with a rest and a nice hot cup of tea,' Professor Ziad said gently as he ushered the bewildered security guard out of the laboratory.

* * * * * * *

'Rutland 6750, Lady Kathleen speaking.'
'I've done it,' Professor Ziad said in pant-wetting jubilation.
'Done what?' Lady Kathleen asked dryly.
'Found the bally elixir of life, that's all,' the over-excited Professor said.
'Well, what are you waiting for? Get around here immediately, and I will tell Sir Ranulf.'
Professor Ziad tried to wrap his coat around Dora, who said, 'It's quite alright, old chap, I can walk.'
Professor Ziad picked up the phial he had marked 'Isobel' and carefully placed it in his pocket. Then he and Dora, the singing duck, walked side by side down the stairs and out of the front door of the C.I.L.I.S.O.D headquarters, getting unusual, strange looks. Pointing and laughing followed as they both got into his mini and drove at full speed to Rutland.

* * * * * * *

'We have enough wind now,' PAL said.
'Well, if it was wind you wanted, we could have asked Legion and Legend,' Jonny said, holding his nose.

'Well, that smell isn't us; it's the antispodackythingy,' Legend said. 'Aspidoceleon,' Jonny replied.

'Yes, that's what I said,' Legend replied.

'No, you didn't; you said antiploppypooppahplumbnuts,' Legion said, giggling.

'Ok, everyone, hold on, we're just about to be jettisoned,' PAL said.

'Jettisoned out of the butt hole of a prehistoric monster, and all before breakfast,' Jonny replied, giggling.

Suddenly, the Silver Arrow Spaceship started to sway violently from side to side, up and down and then began to spin faster and faster, leaving the occupants holding on for dear life as Legend and Legion tried hard not to be sick.

'How much longer?' Jonny shouted to PAL.

'Unsure, as there's so much trapped wind in here. I don't think this monster has been able to break wind for centuries; there seems to be something trapped.' PAL managed to manoeuvre the Silver Arrow Spaceship into a position where he could use the futuristic heat-seeking technology to scan what was causing the blockage.

'Just as I feared, he has a large fish stuck in his butt.'

'Ouch, now that's going to hurt,' Legend said, giggling.

'Not half as much as when it comes out,' PAL replied, then added, 'ok, I'm going to help this poor animal by firing a couple of small laser beams into the blockage.'

PAL fired, and in a millisecond, the blocked fish dissipated, and suddenly, the Aspidoceleon parped a parp so loud it resembled the sound of a million thunderstorms. The Silver Arrow Spaceship and a hurricane of parps left the poor monster's butt in a whoosh of incredible force. PAL flew to the base of the Cliffs at the end of the Earth and then reminded Jonny of all the different types of runes he had to collect.

'They are numbered, but not as in English numbers one to thirteen, but each rune has a mark, the first one has one mark, the second, two marks, the third three marks and so on to thirteen, understood Jonny?'

'Yeah, and then I give them to the Queen of Iceland?'

'No, you bring them back here and keep them safe. Why do you think Legend and Legion are going with you?'

'Yes, I did wonder,' Jonny replied.

'Remember the thirteen Icelandic weird people?' PAL reminded Jonny.

'Oh, I wish I could forget them, but how could I? I mean, how could anyone forget Gattepefur, the doorway sniffer?' Jonny replied, laughing.

'Well, they want the runes, and if they manage to get their grubby little hands on them, you will never get them back. When I say you will never get them back, I mean you will never. Failure to collect the thirteen runes will sadly mean that this will be a failed adventure as all the artefacts you have collected over the past year or so are, for an excellent reason.'

'Yes, I was wondering the same thing,' Jonny replied, then added, 'but I wonder what?'

'Some kind of machine?' Legend asked.

'In time, you will find out, but right now, Jonny, you must begin your search.

* * * * * * *

Without warning, Jonny suddenly found himself on the black volcanic sands at the base of a cliff face. The Cliffs at the end of the Earth looked pretty impressive from inside the warmth and safety of the spaceship, but outside, in the extreme wind and cold, they looked enormous. Jonny leaned back to survey the enormity of these mile-high cliffs and almost fell backwards into the huge waves as they crashed onto the blackened sand with an almighty roar.
Jonny felt very alone as he tightened his belt, double-knotted the old laces on his flimsy plimsolls, and readied himself for the climb. He carefully checked for footholds. He knew the route he had to take and where to find the first rune; however, he didn't expect what happened next. He felt a cold chill on his neck — a very, very cold chill — and a stench he recognised. Slowly, he turned around and almost passed out when he saw what was behind him.
'Thanks for that; I mean, thanks for removing that dead fish from my butt. Oh my God, that was sore and the wind. I thought I was going to die. That fish jumped into my wide-open mouth while I was yawning. I told him to get out, get out your horrible brute, I screamed, but would he? No, he just refused to move, and there's me in all my stunning beauty, trying to keep pretty and what's inside my mouth, yes, a stupid, stupid fish. I mean, what's a girl supposed to do? Well, you know, I coughed,

and I spat, and I choked, and you know Jonny, it would not budge, so I had no choice but to swallow. Anyway, I mustn't stop you from doing whatever it is you think you're doing, and I must fly, but I just wanted to say thank you for clearing my butt. Oh, what a relief, oh sorry, where are my manners? My name is Mary the Mincing Aspidoceleon because I like to mince, as all proper bottom dwellers do in the sea.'

'Bu bu but you're enormous, I mean huge, I mean, oh I don't know what I mean, bu, bu, but you talk, and you talk in English, and you're also, just ever so slightly, err feminine for a monster, especially for a bottom-dwelling sea monster, if you don't mind me saying so, Mary,' Jonny replied unable to close his mouth as his jaw was still resting on the black volcanic sand.

'Do you know what my favourite colour is?' Mary asked, but before Jonny could answer, 'It's pink with a fusion of light blue. Oh, it is so divine and matches my broody eyes. Oh, I love your eyes. What have you done with your hair? Oh, it's the universe, and oh my, you are just so adorable. Now, as I was saying, must fly, byeeeeeeeeeee.' Mary turned and headed back out into the vast stormy seas.

'What the!' Jonny whispered, 'a mincing monster, well that's a first.'

Jonny chuckled to himself and began to climb. 'Jonny, the girls wanted to say hello,' Mary said in that effeminate voice while breathing down Jonny's neck. Jonny turned to see Mary had brought all her girlfriends to meet Jonny. 'Hellooooooooooooooooooooooooow,' they all said in one colossal voice.

'Oh, isn't he just divine? I could gobble him up all by myself,' one of the monsters said in a very sultry but oddly deep, dark voice.

'Oh, don't mind her; she has no moral compass. We call her drag-on queen,' Mary said gently, adding, 'Now we really must go. Jonny has to do some climbing. Why? Well, who knows, so climb away, Jonny and if you ever need nine mincing monsters, go cooeeeeeeeeeee, and we'll be right here.'

Jonny stood in utter disbelief, his jaw wide open and still stuck to the black sands in shock, as he watched these nine gigantic mincing monsters swim back into the stormy seas.

'Right, where was I?' Jonny asked himself, as he gathered his senses and began the vertical, near suicidal - you would have to be insane to even think about attempting this - climb.

Jonny climbed surprisingly quickly and found that the footholds were evenly spaced and perfect for his little hands. Soon, he found himself one hundred yards up, and the higher he climbed, the windier it got and the colder it blew. Suddenly, thousands upon thousands of Common Guillemots appeared out of nowhere using appalling language. No wonder they are called common, Jonny said to himself as they flew a bit too close for comfort while unleashing barrages of abuse. Then thousands of Puffins arrived, but unlike the Common Guillemots, they were refined, polite and ever so courteous. One even asked Jonny if he was alright.

'Yes, yes, I'm fine,' Jonny replied out of breath.

'I hope you don't mind me asking, but what are you doing climbing this ridiculously high and dangerous cliff?' the same polite Puffin asked.

'Oh, I have to collect thirteen Runes, but only one from this, as you say, ridiculously high cliff face,' Jonny replied.

'Well, why didn't you say so? I have it in my nest. I'll go and fetch it for you,' the ever so polite puffin said as she flew away, returning in a few seconds, and in her beak was a PRUNE.

'No, not a prune, a Rune,' Jonny shouted in exasperation.

'Sorry, I couldn't quite hear what you said; you know all the wind,' the ever-so-polite Puffin said, instantly flying off again.

'Oh, that's alright,' Jonny replied, smirking, as he hung on to the side of the highest cliffs in the world while conversing with a Puffin.

'Here it is,' the polite Puffin said as she dropped it into Jonny's hand. Jonny inspected it, half expecting it to be another or the same prune, but hey presto, Jonny had his first rune, and as he held it, it began to flash slowly, just like the Golden Globe did.

'Excuse me, but what's your name?' Jonny asked the polite Puffin.

'Penelope,' the ever so polite Puffin replied, then added, 'Oh, and watch out for Gryla, she's mad bad and dangerous to know,' as Penelope flew back to her nest.

'Penelope, the ever so polite Puffin,' Jonny whispered, his voice filled with fondness, as he bid her a cheerful farewell. He carefully tucked the flashing Rune into his newly sewn inside pocket, a clever precaution he had taken the night before to

ensure the Runes remained safe and secure.
Clever, huh!

Jonny, initially fearless, began to feel a growing
sense of dread as he ascended. The rock face,
once a mere challenge, now loomed before him,
steep, treacherous, and intimidating.

'Small steps,' he repeated, 'small steps.' Sweat
began to pour from his face; his little legs ached
so badly, and his skinny arms screamed for a rest.
But he knew if he stopped, he would never reach
the top. The wind howled and then began to rain,
and when I say rain, I mean the nastiest, meanest,
angriest, coldest, evilest and wettest rain the
weather could conjure up. Clouds suddenly
appeared, rushing at him as if driven by some
malevolent force. Soon surrounded, visibility was
down to zero. Jonny was now climbing blind and
had never been so scared in his sweet, short life.
The rain continued to lash down, but then, he
heard the steady rumble of thunder and a crack of
lightning so powerful and so bright it almost
blinded Jonny and so loud it nearly made him slip.
Jonny held on desperately with one hand, and
using all his superhuman strength, he managed to
get both feet and his other hand back onto the
sheer, slippery cliff, still in total darkness. To
Jonny's horror, the thunder was getting closer and
closer, moving at incredible speed as the lightning
smashed into the rocks below, to the side of him
and above him. Jonny stopped as tears of fear
trickled down his face alongside the torrents of
water cascading down the grey, slippery rock face.
Jonny felt hopeless, alone, and weak when
suddenly, he felt a powerful force that took his

breath away as he was pulled skywards at incredible force and speed.

As Jonny's vision slowly returned, he found himself on solid ground, still drenched and disoriented. In a blink, the thunderstorm vanished, the lightning subsided, and the dark clouds dispersed. Before he stood Legend, Legion, and the Silver Arrow Spaceship, their forms shimmering in the gentle morning light, a sight that filled him with awe and wonder.

'Took your time,' Legend said, yawning, while Legion walked over and allowed Jonny to bury his cold body into the warmth of Legion's colossal body.

'Well, that's the first rune found and secured. If the rest of this journey is going to be as frightening and pant-wetting bad as that,' Jonny said, pointing down the mile-high cliffs at the end of the Earth, 'I'm not too sure that I can do this.'

Jonny's wet clothes soon dried as he took the first Rune out of his secret pocket to show Legend and Legion, who weren't that impressed.

'Is that it? You climbed a sheer cliff face through a thunderstorm just for that?' Legend said, pointing at the small round Rune that continued to flash just like the Golden Globe.

'Why don't you leave it in the Silver Arrow Spaceship?' Legion asked.

'Well blow me, Legion, that's the most sensible thing you have ever suggested,' Legend said.

'Yes, it was rather clever, wasn't it?' Legion replied with pride etched on his face.

* * * * * * *

Jonny placed the first Rune onto a unique floating table, removed the battered old map from his pocket, and placed it on the floor. He then checked to see where the map would take him next and to the second Rune.

'Mmmm, looks like quite a walk, boys,' Jonny said, pointing at the old map.

'So along this winding path, cross that river, swim in that river, walk over that volcanic field, then along another winding path, then climb that glacier, find that huge cave behind that huge scary-looking waterfall, meet the snake with the lisp and stammer, then find the hidden cave, and then find the Queen of Iceland, and sing her this song in either English or Icelandic or both, while dodging the Angka's, the Hairy Growlers, the Greedy Gobblers, the sea monster, ah the sea monster, met him, or was it her, anyway, yes met the Aspidoceleon...'

'Met who? The sea monster?' Legend and Legion said at precisely the same time, interrupting Jonny mid-sentence.

'Oh yes, Mary the Mincing Aspidoceleon and his mincing friends,' Jonny replied, giggling.

'Well, weren't you frightened?' Legend asked.

'What of Mary the Mincing Aspidoceleon and his many mincing friends? No, he was brilliant and so friendly.' Jonny replied.

'He? He? He?' Legion stammered.

'Why are you laughing, numbnuts?' Jonny asked, giggling.

'You said Mary the Mincing Aspidoceleon was a he,' Legion said, scratching his enormous head.

'Yes, I did, as Mary was a very friendly sea monster, and so were all his friends; all of them were absolutely wonderful, friendly and ever so grateful and all males.'

'Well, I wasn't expecting that,' Legion replied.

'No, nor was I, now, where was I? Oh yes, the Huldufock or the Hidden People, the Lagarfljot Worm, Trolls, and be home by teatime, no doubt,' Jonny folded the battered old map, placed it back in his backpack and asked, 'OK, are we ready to meet a lisping stuttering five-mile-long snake?'

'No, no, we are not,' Legend and Legion replied in unison, 'but for you, we will.'

'I wonder what he is called,' Legion pondered.

'Well, he is called a Lagrfljotsormurnn, so knowing our luck, he's probably called Larry.'

Suddenly, both Legion and Legend's ears pricked up and looked out over the sea.

''Incoming,' PAL said.

Jonny looked out to where both Legend and Legion were staring. Then he heard the faintest noise, like a humming, slowly getting louder and louder. Suddenly, a tiny dot appeared in the skies, and as it got closer, the noise got louder.

'PAL, become invisible,' Jonny shouted, and the Silver Arrow Spaceship immediately disappeared. The noise grew louder and louder until Jonny recognised it as the sound of an old aeroplane - an ancient Lancaster bomber.

'Why would a Second World War aeroplane be flying towards Iceland?' Jonny asked PAL.

'I have scanned the plane, and it has just six occupants: Sir Ranulf, Sir Harry, Eddie Rockhard, and three unknown men,' PAL replied.

'My father? Here, now, but why?' Jonny asked, bewildered.

'No idea,' PAL replied.

'PAL, shouldn't we send them a signal or something?' Jonny asked.

'Yes, good idea. I will send some pulse waves and bring them into the land.'

'Oh, you can do that, can you PAL?' Jonny asked, visibly impressed.

'Just watch.'

Suddenly, a powerful stream of magnetic pulses gently hit the old Lancaster Bomber. PAL then engulfed the enormous plane in a beam of mighty energy, gently bringing it to rest right next to the still-invisible Silver Arrow Spaceship.

'Bally hell, old boy,' Sir Ranulf was heard shouting as the drone of the four giant engines stopped, and the propellers came to a silent halt.

'Bally hell,' Sir Ranulf replied, 'bally, bally, bally hell.'

'Hello, Dad, what are you doing here?' Jonny asked, looking up towards the cockpit where Sir Ranulf and Harry sat, unable to move through fear.

'Bally hell,' Sir Ranulf repeated. Then Sir Harry joined in, 'Bally, bally, bally, bally, bally, bally, bally, bally, hell,' both men repeated, still unable to move or remove their headsets.

Suddenly, the old door on the side of the Lancaster bomber flew open, and Eddie Rockhard stood in the doorway, filling the entire space.

'You alright, laddie?' The gruff Glaswegian mumbled.

'What did he say?' Legend asked.

'Do you wear a bra? I think,' Legion replied, laughing.

'Jonny, you have to go home,' Eddie shouted.

Jonny cupped his hands over his ears, finding it hard to hear Eddie over the wind.

'I said you must go home,' Eddie shouted again.

'I think he said, can you give me a bone,' Legend said, giggling.

Ashen-faced, Sir Ranulf appeared next to Eddie Rockhard and shouted for Jonny to come home. Jonny found it hard to hear him properly, so he ran over to the open doorway where Sir Ranulf knelt and shouted in Jonny's ear.

'Isobel is in a coma; come quick, come now.'

'How did Isobel fall into a coma?' Jonny shouted back.

'Will explain on the way back, so hop in,' Sir Ranulf replied, holding out his huge hands to pull Jonny into the belly of the Lancaster Bomber.

'If Isobel is in a coma, then I need to get back as soon as possible. Where is she?' Jonny shouted.

'Great Ormond Street Hospital, but you must get the one hundred phials first,' Sir Ranulf replied.

'Why?' Jonny shouted.

'To save her life, of course,' Sir Ranulf replied matter-of-factly.

'They don't save lives; they create and improve lives. The only way I can save Isobel is to take her to Jala. Hold on a second,' Jonny rushed into the Silver Arrow Spaceship and asked PAL...

'Can we carry the Lancaster bomber in our energy beams, or is it too dangerous?'

'Yes, of course, we can,' PAL replied.

'Dad, get back into your seats; we'll carry you back. But hold on, all of you, hold on.'

Jonny ran back to the now-visible Silver Arrow Spaceship. The comparison between the two crafts was unbelievable. Jonny smiled as he,

Legend, and Legion jumped into the shimmering Silver Arrow Spaceship through the doorway made of light.

'OK, PAL, do what you must, but please be careful. That cargo in there is just a bit, ever so special.'

PAL turned on the powerful energy beams, which completely engulfed the old Lancaster Bomber. It gently lifted this sixteen-thousand-kilogram monster into the air as if it weighed the same as a feather. Slowly, the Silver Arrow Spaceship turned on its axis. Suddenly, with astonishing speed and a blinding flash of brilliant white light, it was gone, but someone or something was watching.

'Bally hell,' Sir Ranulf shouted through his mouthpiece as they flew towards the tiny landing strip at the speed of light.

'Bally, bally, bally wibble wobble wabble,' Sir Harry replied, giggling as he looked at Eddie Rockhard, where the air pressure played havoc with his lantern-jawed face.

* * * * * * *

'Good grief, we're already home,' an astonished Sir Ranulf said, pointing towards the tiny landing strip below. Gently, the massive Lancaster bomber landed, much to the surprise of just a handful of workers who had prepped the old bomber for this one-off trip. None of them had seen the futuristic spacecraft made entirely from intelligent light before, which hovered almost invisibly in the afternoon sun. Then, much to their amazement, Jonny jumped out from seemingly nowhere to tell Sir Ranulf that he would go straight to Great Ormond Street to see Isobel and disappeared again. In the blink of an eye, this massive Spaceship turned south and, with incredible unseen power, took off with unbelievable acceleration, leaving the ground workers dumbstruck.

'Come on, old boys, you must have seen a futuristic spaceship made entirely from intelligent light before, haven't you?' Sir Ranulf quipped as he climbed down the steps from the belly of the Lancaster Bomber and walked away with Sir Harry, Eddie Rockhard, and the other members of the elite squadron as if this was a daily occurrence. Well, to them, it was, but to the general public, simply a one-off, never-to-be-repeated experience of not only one lifetime but many, many lifetimes.

'Tell your kids,' Sir Harry shouted, 'they won't ever believe you.'

* * * * * * *

Jonny sat with his head bowed in the spotlessly clean Flower Ward of Great Ormond Street Hospital, unable to speak or take his eyes off Isobel as she lay silently in her hospital bed. Plastic breathing tubes drip for this and drip for that - Isobel's breathing was only possible through a massive machine.

'Can't you help? Jonny, can't you help my daughter?' Isobel's mother pleaded with the deadly silent Jonny.

'Please, please help me. She's our only child, Jonny, please. I'm sorry if I said those horrid things about you. Jonny, please, I beg of you, help Isobel.'

Jonny looked at the tear-filled face of Isobel's mother and smiled.

'We had to put her into a medically induced coma,' the nurse whispered to Jonny. 'If we hadn't, her brain would already be of no use, and her life expectancy would be very short.'

The nurse silently closed the door behind her as Jonny touched Isobel's head. He began to sing…

'Wake up my little bluebell,
Awake from your deep sleep,
You know we have a journey,
A promise of love to keep,
Wake up my little shadow,
Awake from your deep sleep,
I will take you on a journey,
A promise of love to keep.'

While singing this song, Jonny began removing the tubes, wires, plastic tubes and breathing equipment.

'Wake up my little bluebell,
Awake from your deep sleep,
You know we have a journey,
A promise of love to keep,
Wake up my little shadow,
Awake from your deep sleep,
I will take you on a journey,
A promise of love to keep.'

'What on earth are you doing?' the nurse said, rushing in as alarm bells rang.

'It's okay, it's okay, he knows what he is doing,' Lady Taylor said gently.

'I am very sorry, but you just cannot remove her life support; she will die,' the nurse growled.

'She will die if I don't,' Jonny replied, continuing to sing in his beautiful voice.

'Wake up my little bluebell,
Awake from your deep sleep.
You know we have a journey,
A promise of love to keep.
Wake up my little shadow,
Awake from your deep sleep.
I will take you on a journey,
A promise of love to keep.'

'Let it be,' Lady Taylor said as she gently held the nurse's arm.

Suddenly, security guards and doctors rushed in as Jonny sang his lullaby.

'Stop him immediately,' one doctor shouted.

'You will have to go through us first,' the grizzled, deep Glaswegian voice of Eddie Rockhard whispered menacingly from the now open door.

Everyone spun round to see Eddie Rockhard, three vast and armed-to-the-teeth soldiers standing alongside Sir Ranulf, Sir Harry, and Sir Taylor.

'And me,' Professor Ziad said, puffing and panting.

'Where have you been?' Sir Ranulf asked the out-of-breath, sweating Professor.

'I thought you were going to find a cure.'

'Well, these medicines are only medicines to help life and improve new ones. Sadly, the best I could do is revive a duck whose neck was badly injured but now can speak in perfect Hebrew,' Professor Ziad replied, smiling.

'Oh, how wonderful. Well, when I need a Hebrew-speaking duck, I'll ring you up,' Sir Ranulf whispered back, then added, 'So where is this Hebrew-speaking duck now?'

'Oh, left her at home, old boy, singing to my wife,' Professor Ziad laughed.

Jonny continued to remove drips from Isobel's silent body as Eddie, the three-armed soldiers Sir Ranulf, Sir Harry, and Sir Taylor formed an impenetrable line of defence around Jonny and Isobel. Lady Taylor openly wept, 'My Isobel, my baby girl.'

Jonny gently lifted the lifeless body of Isobel in his arms, still singing his gentle lullaby to reassure the sleeping Isobel that all was going to be okay.

'Make way for the wee laddy,' Eddie Rockhard said quietly, 'and no sudden moves.'

Jonny walked a few steps towards the door, looked straight to the heavens, and just vanished.

'What the!!!!' a Doctor said in bewilderment, 'where did he go? Call security, call security.'

'We are security,' Eddie Rockhard growled into the doctor's face.

* * * * * * *

'PAL, take us to Jala.' Those were the only words Jonny said as he laid Isobel's lifeless body onto the world's most comfortable, almost invisible bed, as Legend and Legion looked on. Jonny kept singing, repeating the lullaby he knew Isobel could hear.

The Silver Spaceship pointed vertically into the air. With an enormous surge of jaw-dropping, knee-wobbling, pant-wetting power, it left the Great Ormond Street Hospital roof at mind-boggling speed and acceleration.

* * * * * * *

'Let's go home,' Lady Kathleen said as she gently held Lady Taylor's trembling hand.

'I liked the "looks like someone set your face on fire then put it out with a pitchfork," that made me giggle for days,' Lady Taylor said, wiping the tears from her face.

'You know I meant every word,' Lady Kathleen replied, smiling, and together, along with Sir Ranulf, Sir Harry, Sir Taylor, Eddie Rockhard, and the three armed-to-the-teeth special operation soldiers, left Great Ormond Street Hospital the usual way, yes, via the stairs.

* * * * * * *

Jonny sat back and stared at Isobel's sleeping body in silence, hoping beyond hope that there was a cure.

'We need to be quick, Jonny, as now she isn't in a medically induced coma, every second counts,' PAL said as Isobel's lifeless body was scanned by futuristic technology way more advanced than anything they had on Earth.

'Can you fix her for me?' Jonny asked, still holding Isobel's hand.

'Fixed her broken bones,' PAL replied, adding, 'she is comfortable. There are no more broken bones, and I have already fixed her hip, the bruising, and internal bleeding. It's her brain; that's the real issue here. I can only do so much. It's the life-giving pure waters of Jala that this young lady requires, but Jonny,' PAL paused for a second and then said, 'there are no guarantees in this universe or any of the millions of multiverses. Jonny, we must accept and understand the incredible powers beyond us. Sometimes, Jonny, when it's someone's time to leave, we cannot change this; not even the pure waters of Jala can alter life. Isobel may or may not survive, and this harsh reality is something all humans have to learn to accept. All we can do is accept that this was Isobel's wish.'

'To die?' Jonny asked, with tears welling up in his eyes.

'Yes, Jonny, to die and then to be reborn. This is how life works and has been since life began.'

Jonny sang his lullaby to Isobel as they sped through the far reaches of space at three hundred and sixty thousand miles per second.

'Wake up my little bluebell,

Awake from your deep sleep.

You know we have a journey,

A promise of love to keep.

Wake up my little shadow,

Awake from your deep sleep.

I will take you on a journey,

A promise of love to keep.'

Within minutes, PAL announced they were nearly at Jala, the Planet of Pure Water.

Legend said, 'Remember your prayer, Jonny. It might come in handy when you enter the pure waters.'

'Yes, good idea, Legend, good idea,' Jonny replied, still holding onto Isobel's delicate hand while not taking his eyes off her for a second.

'Best you prepare yourself, Jonny, as we are almost there,' PAL said.

Jonny fell to his knees, and in the prayer position, he quietly and silently prayed to the powers of the multiverse to help Isobel get better.

'Legend and Legion will be joining you, and they also need the powers of the life-giving waters of Jala,' PAL said quietly. Now, are you all ready?'

'Yes,' they all replied in unison. Jonny picked up Isobel's body and stood silently, waiting for the fastest rollercoaster ride in the universe, straight down at breakneck speed. In an instant, all four were waist-high in the most beautiful, tranquil, stunningly serene, pure waters of Jala.

In the distance, Jonny saw two magnificent water horses galloping towards him. They were a sight of truly incredible beauty as they ran in silence, vast waves of multi-coloured water producing enormous plumes and sprays of iridescent colours that took one's breath away. Jonny stood transfixed and then looked to the heavens to see millions upon millions of stars as the pure waters of Jala lapped against his body.

Starshell and Firestorm arrived in a wave of splashing water, soaking Jonny, Legend, Legion and the still-sleeping Isobel.

'Place Isobel on my back,' Firestorm said gently as he knelt. Jonny carefully laid Isobel's body on Firestorm's vast, muscular, multi-coloured back, ensuring she could not fall off.

'Swim with us,' Starshell said gently, 'swim with us, let go of all emotions and feelings, and think only of purity. Think of cleansing thoughts. Consider removing every sickness and illness in yourself and, most importantly, for Isobel. Think about removing every bad, negative, and angry thought. Let go, everyone, let go.'

Jonny felt every wound, scar and pain being healed and revitalised in his body. Legend and Legion basked in the calmness and serenity of the moment as their bodies again grew stronger and stronger.

'Now we must all concentrate on Isobel,' Firestorm said as they swam together in the life-giving waters.

'Jonny, now please recite your prayers in Aramaic.'

'Aboon dabashmaya
(Our Father in Heaven)
Nethkadash shamak
(Holy is thy name)
Tetha malkoothak
(Your kingdom is coming)
Newe tzevyanak
(Your will be done)
AYKAN DABASHMAYA
(On Earth as it is in heaven)
AF BARA HAV LAN LAKMA DSOONKANAN
(Give us bread for our needs day by day)
Yamana washbook lan
(Forgive us our offences)
KAVINE AIKANA DAF
(As we have forgiven our offenders)
HANAN SHABOOKAN IHAYAVINE OOLOW TALAHN LANESYANA
(Do not let us enter into temptation)
ELA FATSAN MEN BEESHA'
(Deliver us from error).

'Now, Jonny, sing your lullaby,' Starshell added.
'How did you know about the lullaby?' a very relaxed Jonny asked.

'We know more than you could ever imagine,'
Firestorm replied.

Jonny cleared his throat and began to sing his
little lullaby to Isobel...

'Wake up, my little bluebell
Awake from your deep sleep
You know we have a journey
A promise of love to keep
Please wake up, my little shadow
Awake from your deep sleep
I will take you on a journey
A promise of love to keep.'

'What would you give for Isobel to be well again?'
Starshell asked as they swam in pure, beautiful
water, 'Would you give your life?'

'Yes,' Jonny replied without a second's hesitation.

'Why?' Firestorm asked.

'I am unsure why, but I believe it would be the
right thing to do.'

'But Jonny, what about your life and that of your
family and friends? What about Legend and
Legion? What about your future, Jonny?' Starshell
asked.

'Isobel would do the same for me,' Jonny replied.

'Yes, Jonny, she would; she was willing to give
everything up so you can live, Jonny. Not many
people on your world called Earth would so
happily give their life for someone else. Nanny
Noo gave her entire life to help your mother and to
save others,' Starshell said gently. Jonny, fearing
the worst, raised his voice in the quiet and solitude
of the pure waters of Jala.

'No, no, please, Isobel, don't do this, we can
survive together, we can, we can,' Jonny
whimpered as he believed that Isobel had already

given her life and soul so that Jonny could live and save the world from sin.

'Jonny,'

'Yes, Firestorm,'

'She lives.'

Like any child his age, Jonny, irrespective of his courage, strength, and honesty, cried a million tears of joy that dripped effortlessly into the pure waters, sending ripples cascading across the vast seas.

'Thank you,' Jonny whispered, 'thank you.' 'Now close your eyes,' Firestorm said gently. Jonny closed his eyes and.......

To be continued...